ESCAPE THE VIRUS

A POST-APOCALYPTIC SURVIVAL THRILLER -
LAST PANDEMIC BOOK 1

RYAN WESTFIELD

1

MATT

It was just another day at the office for Matt. Another boring day where nothing ever seemed to happen. Another day where Matt had to fight the urge to leave and never come back.

He'd often wondered how he'd gotten himself into this mess, how he'd managed to let his debt pile up the way it had, putting him in a financial position where he simply couldn't afford to leave.

Matt needed the job. That was reality.

"Did you get a chance to take a look at those spreadsheets?" said McGovern, the assistant to the manager.

McGovern had a way of standing too close to Matt. Matt used his feet to discreetly move his rolling chair a couple inches to the left. But, as if aware of the maneuver, McGovern absentmindedly took another step in Matt's direction, once again closing the gap between them.

"Uh, I was about to do them," said Matt.

"That's what you told me yesterday."

"Well, I really mean it this time. Don't worry. Look, I'll pull them up right now."

McGovern actually stood there and watched as Matt pulled up the email, opened the spreadsheet, and started scrolling through the hundreds of columns, pretending to really examine it.

"I'll take it from here," said Matt, not bothering to hide the annoyance in his voice.

McGovern muttered something as he left, no doubt off to breathe down someone else's neck.

Matt hated it. The whole setup. He hated having a boss like that. He hated feeling like a little kid who hadn't done his chores.

It wasn't that he hated authority, or had a problem obeying orders. Well, maybe just a little. He had, after all, been a little rebellious back in school.

But, overall, he'd respect authority as long as the authority figure earned his respect first.

His current bosses hadn't earned his respect. In fact, it seemed that they'd done their best to prove they weren't worthy of any respect.

The spreadsheet in question, for instance, had already been looked over by Matt at least ten times. His bosses just kept sending it back to him, asking him to review it, apparently forgetting that he was the author of the whole document. They were just too disorganized, too focused on their own little promotions, to actually get any efficient work done.

"Psst, Matt," someone hissed.

Matt looked up and saw his buddy Damian's face peering at him from down the long desk that they all sat at.

How pathetic was it that they didn't even have cubicles, or their own private desks?

"What?" hissed Matt, back at him. He didn't want

McGovern to come back over. He didn't need any more shit today than he was already due.

Larry, an older, permanently disgruntled guy, shot Matt a harsh look.

"Check your email," Damian hissed.

Not wanting to get hissed at any more, risking McGovern's attention, Matt did what his friend told him to do. He checked his email.

Among the dozen or so pointless work-related emails, there was a message that had been forwarded from Damian.

Matt opened the email. There was no subject line. And the body of the email contained only a link.

Matt clicked it. It took him to a news site. Just a regular one. Mainstream.

The headline was larger than normal. Or so it seemed. Maybe it was just a trick of the eye.

"H77 VIRUS PROVEN DEADLY IN 85% OF POPULATION," ran the headline.

Matt felt his heart start to beat a little faster as he read through the article.

It wasn't the first time he'd heard of the H77 virus. But it was the first time he'd heard that it was so deadly.

He vaguely remembered hearing something about H77 in the news a couple weeks ago, while at the barber shop, but then it had seemed as if it would just be another one of the yearly hyped-up threats. Nothing too serious. Nothing to really worry about.

For a while now, it seemed as if every year there was some new virus that the media outlets made a big deal of. Several years back it had been the swine flu. And there'd been the bird flu, of course.

For a while, it had seemed like all the viruses would be named after animals.

Matt stood up, his swivel chair rolling backwards away from him.

"Wasn't that article crazy, man?" said Damian, who was already pushing past him, headed towards the break room. "What the hell is going on in there anyway?"

"Don't know," said Matt, following Damian quickly into the break room.

In the break room, there was just one person. Someone who worked on another floor. A man that Matt recognized but didn't know. Maybe he'd exchanged a few words with him once or twice.

The man was standing right in front of the TV, which was mounted high in the corner of the little room. He was gazing up at it, completely transfixed.

"What's all this shouting about?" said McGovern, stepping into the room behind Matt and Damian. "People are trying to work in here. There are spreadsheets to look over. Clients to attend to!"

"Remember that H77 virus?" said the man who'd shouted, without taking his eyes off the TV.

"What's that got to do with anything?" said McGovern. "You're disturbing the peace and calm. People have to work, you know. Just where do you get the nerve..."

"I never thought it would actually happen," said the man, completely ignoring McGovern. "I always thought these stories were silly... but they said that an entire 747 from Beijing, arriving at JFK, was contaminated..."

"Contaminated? With what?" said Matt, his mind jumping to the article he'd just read.

There'd been details in the article that he'd just skipped over. The country of origin of the virus, for instance.

The news anchor answered his question for him. "The H77 virus," she was saying. "Is considered by experts to be have characteristics that make it especially threatening to our national security. The reports we've been getting indicate that the virus has a completely silent incubation period of two days. That means that before any symptoms show up, the virus will have time to spread, because during those two days, it is highly contagious."

The room had filled up. It seemed as if the whole office had packed themselves into the little break room.

Matt was standing shoulder-to-shoulder with people he didn't immediately recognize.

The room was deathly quiet except for the TV news anchor.

"We have here an expert on the subject of viruses... Dr. Jacob...."

The TV announcer seemed a little flustered, and things weren't moving as smoothly as they normally did on the news.

Matt got the impression that they were sort of throwing this program together on the fly.

The view suddenly shifted to a different camera, showing a close-up of the face of a man in his late fifties. He had gray, wavy hair that was swept back, a short goatee. He wore a tweed sports coat with patches on the elbows. He looked every inch the professor.

"So you were saying that it's as if this virus was designed to be lethal to the largest number of people possible?" came the anchor's voice, off camera.

"They really screwed up this shot," muttered Damian.

A couple of people shushed him somewhat violently.

"Yes, that's right," said the professor. The camera was zooming in even more. On the flat-screen TV, each of his oversized pores was clearly visible. "What we're looking at here is a perfect killing machine... As far as we know, there are absolutely no symptoms during the two-day dormancy period in which the virus happens to be highly contagious... and I should mention that we don't know everything we should know about this virus. It's entirely possible that symptoms in some people will show up earlier, rather than later..."

"And how exactly is the virus transmitted?" said the off-screen female voice, cutting off the professor's explanation.

"We're not yet sure, but it's highly likely that the virus is airborne..."

"This is crazy," Damian was muttering.

Matt silently agreed. It definitely was crazy. He tore his eyes away from the TV screen and looked around the room.

His coworkers were typical office workers. Many were out of shape and overweight. Their eyes were completely fixated on the TV screen. Their faces showed rapt attention mixed with fear and terror.

Matt didn't know whether they'd understand the full consequences of this or not. Somehow, he doubted it. Just because their faces showed fear didn't mean they understood.

Matt's own mind was racing as he put the pieces together. There were so many possibilities. So many ways it could all go wrong.

He needed to be alone. He needed to think. To figure this out.

He knew that this was extremely serious, but he had already heard enough from the TV. He knew what he needed to know.

Matt turned around, and began pushing his way through the crowd.

Everyone was so close, so packed together. It was difficult to push through them. People gave him nasty looks as they stepped out of the way for him.

Elbows jostled him. Someone stepped on his foot. Someone heavy.

Matt had never feared tight spaces or crowds. But now, with the threat of a deadly virus on his mind, the density of the crowd seemed almost intolerable.

"Sorry, coming through," Matt kept saying, over and over again.

Finally, he was almost to the door.

"We've had some reports that this could be a weaponized virus, but as of yet this is still unconfirmed. I repeat, this is unconfirmed..."

There was only one more person to push past before Matt was out of the break room.

"Excuse me," he muttered.

Then he saw her.

Jamie.

She looked just as good as she had on their last date, one month ago.

They'd been quite the pair in the office, flirting over the course of a year, before he'd finally asked her out. People like Damian had asked him what had taken him so long. Matt hadn't responded, but his real reason was that he hadn't wanted to mess up the office environment if things didn't work out.

But he'd eventually caved and asked her out anyway.

And, now, after their third date had ended in what could only be called a quiet disaster, he realized his fears had been well founded.

Since those dates, they hadn't spoken. In fact, they hadn't even looked at each other. It was safe to say they weren't on good terms.

Jamie didn't meet his gaze, and she stepped to the side, giving Matt a wide berth.

"Thanks," he muttered, knowing she wouldn't respond.

He breathed a sigh of relief as he got through the doorway, finding himself back in the regular office space.

OK, it was time to do some quick thinking.

Matt pulled out his cell phone. Opened the calculator app.

How many people were there on a 747? About 400 or 500, most likely. The exact numbers didn't matter so much.

If the virus was as contagious as they said it was, maybe they were right about everyone being infected.

So 500 people arrived in New York. Then they dispersed. Some of them went home via taxi, private car, or subway...

How many people would someone contaminate on the subway? Matt tried to imagine the last time he'd been on the NYC subway, thinking about how many people he'd been up close to. It had been rush hour. He didn't know the answer, but it had been a lot. A lot of people.

And what about those people who got on connecting flights?

Matt's office was in Albuquerque, where he'd lived for the last five years. He knew that there had to be at least a dozen daily flights from JFK to Albuquerque.

So what were the chances that someone had gotten off that Beijing flight and arrived in Albuquerque?

They seemed pretty high to Matt. After all, Albuquerque was a major hub for business in the western states.

And if someone hadn't made that particular trip? With two asymptomatic-yet-contagious days the virus would spread fast enough to get to Albuquerque in no time. And not just Albuquerque. It would spread all over the United States.

But, wait, what if he was overreacting?

What if they'd already rounded up everyone who'd been on that plane?

"And the passengers on flight J832 have not yet been notified?" came the anchor's TV voice from inside the break room.

"That's correct," came the expert's voice. "To the best of my knowledge, none of them have been notified."

None of them had even been *notified*? That sounded completely insane. They should have been quarantined, not just notified.

Matt's heart was beating much faster than usual.

His mind was racing.

He'd always been a practical-minded man, and with just his own common sense, he knew that this was going to be bad.

Very bad.

If he wanted to live, he had to act.

And soon.

Matt knew that whatever the people on the news told the public, it wouldn't be enough. He'd seen it time and time again. Whoever was in charge always managed to screw it all up.

He'd have to think for himself. Find his own way. Think things through himself. Not rely on anyone else.

2

"So he just walked past you and didn't say anything?" said Mia.

"I think he mumbled something, but no, he didn't really say anything."

"And you didn't say anything either?"

"I just didn't know what to say."

Jamie was back in her apartment, talking with her roommate of two years, Mia.

Jamie had been sent home from work earlier, along with all the other employees.

The whole city was on lockdown. Some type of new emergency quarantine status that the mayor had made up. Cities across the country had done the same.

Mia hadn't gone to work at all today, although no matter what Jamie asked, Mia didn't seem capable of offering up a simple easy-to-understand answer. But that's just the way Mia was. She wasn't exactly "practically" minded, which sometimes annoyed Jamie to no end.

Jamie was anxious to change the subject away from Matt. In fact, she wished that she hadn't even mentioned their brief little "non-encounter" at the office today. After all, there were bigger things to worry about.

"Anything else on the news?" she asked.

Mia, who had been staring at her cell phone during the entire conversation, shook her head. "Nope," she said. "Just more of the same. They've found about thirty of the passengers... got them to the hospitals... quarantined and everything..."

"And the other... how many are there?"

"Uh, 323, I think. It wasn't quite a full flight."

"Yeah. The other 323. What about them? They didn't find them?"'

"Nope. Not yet. They're still out there. It's all everyone online is talking about."

"Wait, are you on actual news sites, or are you just looking at social media?"

"Uh, social media... But it's just as good."

"You can't get all your news from social media. Come on, Mia, that's crazy."

"What's the difference? Look, here are a bunch of quotes from CBS. So you know it's real."

"I'm going to pull it up myself.

Jamie was already tired of staring at her phone, but she took it out again, and pulled up a couple of different news sites.

"I just don't get why they haven't contacted the other... what is it... 323? How hard could it be?"

"You know how it is," said Mia. "Nothing ever goes as planned... Things are always harder than they seem to be on paper. Like take you and Matt, for instance. On paper, you and Matt made such a great pair. And then what happened? You only lasted three dates. And you still won't even tell me what happened."

Jamie rolled her eyes. "Can we drop it?" she said. "There's a national emergency going on. We're on lockdown with the rest of the city, and all you can think about is me and my three dates with my coworker."

"Whatever," muttered Mia.

There was a knock on the door.

Jamie and Mia exchanged a look.

"I'll get it," said Jamie, getting up.

She and Mia lived in a fairly large apartment building in a decent section of downtown Albuquerque. Like many people who lived in large apartment buildings, she didn't know any of her neighbors. She might have recognized a couple of people, but she didn't know any names.

Jamie paused before the answering the door, realizing that she didn't know who was on the other side.

She looked around, searching for something that she could defend herself with, if it was needed. She needed some sort of weapon, but she didn't see anything that would remotely do the job.

She settled on a small lamp that Mia had purchased online, unpacked, and then left on the floor. Jamie figured it was better than nothing. She took it in her right hand, and, opening the door with her left just a crack, managed to keep the lamp out of sight.

There was no peephole on the door. But it had never been a problem before. After all, people didn't typically come to the door. Packages were delivered to the mailboxes on the first floor.

"Hello?" said Jamie.

A man stared back at her. About fifty years old. Gray hair, and a big gray beard.

He wore a slightly rumpled suit, and had an expensive-looking watch on. He looked like a lawyer who had been putting in too many all-nighters recently.

He was breathing quickly, and there was some sweat beading up on his forehead.

"Hey," he said, speaking in a quick, harried way. "Come on. Let's go. We've got to get out of here. They're evacuating the building."

"They're what?"

"What's going on out there?" called out Mia from the other room.

"They're evacuating the building. I don't know why."

"But what about the emergency curfew? It's city-wide. We're supposed to stay inside no matter what."

"Yeah, because of the virus, I know. But these guys want us out of here. I think it's a gas leak or something."

Jamie was eyeing the man, who was glancing around nervously, eyes dancing up and down the hall. It looked like he was afraid of something. He looked like he had something to hide.

She suddenly caught a whiff of his breath. It stank like he'd been drinking heavily.

She clutched the lamp tighter, and brought it a little closer to herself, meanwhile closing the door about another inch. "Where did you say you lived?" she said. "I don't remember seeing you before."

"Right over there," he said, pointing vaguely down the hall. "I recognize you. Come on. Let's go. We've got to go."

He reached forward, as if to grab her, but he pulled his arm back at the last moment.

"Where's everybody else?" said Jamie, her suspicions growing by the second.

Could it be that this drunk man was using the quarantine lockdown as an opportunity to do something unsavory?

What should she do?

She had half a mind to shut the door in his face.

But what if he was right? What if there really was a gas leak. She didn't smell anything, but that didn't mean there couldn't be a big one in the basement, making the building extremely dangerous to inhabit.

There had been, after all, a gas leak about six months ago. She'd had to evacuate with everyone else while the city gas company investigated. In the end, they'd said it had been close to exploding.

"Mia? Would you come here?"

Calling Mia wasn't much use, but she didn't know what else to do.

Suddenly, the fire alarm sounded. It was the whole-building alarm.

About ten seconds later, the sprinklers in the hall started spraying water, rotating jerkily.

Someone appeared at the far end of the hall. He yelled something unintelligible, and then raced down the stairs.

"Come on!" the guy at the doorway was more urgent than ever.

It seemed like he might be telling the truth after all.

"Mia! Come on. We've got to go. Grab your phone."

"What is it?" said Mia, appearing at her side in what seemed like an instant.

"Come on. You have your keys?"

"Yeah."

Jamie grabbed Mia's hand, pulled her through the doorway, and closed the door hard behind them.

Jamie's hair was already getting wet as she pushed past the drunk man and pulled Mia along with her down the hallway.

"What did that guy want? What's going on?"

"They're evacuating the building. Gas leak."

"But we're supposed to..."

Jamie already knew what Mia was going to say. But as she often did, she felt like she had to play the big sister role to Mia, and get her to safety.

In the few minutes that it took to get to the main entrance, Jamie and Mia were both soaking wet.

The main entrance hall was crowded with people. The fire alarm had drawn them all out of their apartments.

Jamie kept a tight hold of Mia's hand and started pushing through the crowd of people.

"Excuse me, excuse me," she kept saying, but everyone ignored her, and she had to actually push people aside.

Why were they going so slow?

Didn't they understand how serious a gas leak was?

She still didn't like the idea of that sweating man in the suit, and she kept glancing over her shoulder, trying to see if he had followed them.

"Here we go," Jamie muttered, as she pushed her way through to the outside.

Mia was right behind her.

It was a day in early spring, and, as sometimes happened, it had started off sunny but had turned gray and somewhat dark.

It wasn't even late afternoon yet, but it looked as if the day were almost over. Ominous dark rain clouds hung in the sky, having rolled in from the mountains nearby. Of course, a lot of the time they'd roll off just as readily, leaving a sunny day once again in their wake.

In the semi-darkness, blue and red lights flashed and sirens wailed.

Two large firetrucks were parked in front of the building, as well as a few police cars.

A policeman was standing on the sidewalk, megaphone in hand. "Move away from the building. Move away from the building, please," he was saying over and over again, static hissing through his monotone words.

The policeman wore what looked like a cheap poncho, as well as a white surgical mask over his face. Despite the clouds, he wore large sunglasses, making almost the entirety of his face hidden.

Somehow, the whole scene sent a chill through Jamie. Her heart was thumping away in her chest, and it felt like there was a lump in her throat.

"What's going on?" said Mia. Normally somewhat divorced from reality, it was apparent from her tone of voice that she was frightened by the scene that was unfolding. "Are they wearing those masks because of the virus?"

"Must be."

"It looks creepy."

Jamie and Mia moved off to the side, towards the sidewalk. It seemed as if every time Jamie turned her head, she saw another cop. They were swarming the place, and they were all wearing surgical masks and cheap-looking raincoats.

People were still streaming out of the apartment building's main entrance.

Despite all the commotion, all the sirens and the crowd, the rest of the street was desolate. Not a car drove by and not a person could be seen walking. There were other apartment buildings within sight, but apparently everyone was remaining inside.

"You think this was really a gas leak?" said Mia.

Jamie didn't answer. She was too busy scanning the area, trying to understand the situation. She always liked to be informed, to understand her position.

Nearby, two cops were talking. "Do they really think these masks are going to do anything? I heard the virus particles are so small it doesn't matter. It'll go through everything except the serious filters... you know, the really fine ones..."

"And what about these ponchos?" muttered the other cop. "What the hell are these supposed to do? I doubt it'd work on a drizzle, let alone the deadliest virus ever to grace humanity... If only the department had bought some decent gear last year when they had the chance... these things look like they came from the hardware store."

"I think they actually did. We're screwed," said the other cop. "Let's just admit it."

"Nah, we've seen worse. Come on, this is just another big to-do about nothing..."

Jamie's eyes had been following the cops as they talked. One of them now looked over at her, catching her eye, and she quickly looked away down at her feet, avoiding his gaze.

"Hey, Jamie," hissed Mia. "Look at that." She pointed off to the other side of the street.

Two large vans had just pulled up. They looked like Mercedes Sprinter vans, based on how tall they were. Jamie knew the model, since some of her friends had been thinking about buying them to convert into small RV dwellings.

There were no markings on the vans, but something about them seemed official. Maybe it was the way they were parked.

Then the doors of both opened in unison. Two people stepped out of each van.

But they barely looked like people.

They were suited up in the sort of gear that Jamie had only seen in the movies. The suits looked like a cross between a surgeon's outfit and a scuba diver's gear. Their faces weren't visible. Thick goggles obscured their eyes.

No doubt those were the types of suits that the chatting cops would have liked to have.

Jamie knew what it was. It was some type of team that dealt with contagious viruses. Each city of a decent size probably had at least one clandestine unit like this.

"I don't like the looks of this," muttered Mia, as they watched the four heavily suited individuals make their way slowly towards the apartment building. They wore tanks on their backs, and towed little wagons behind them. At the curb, they had to stop and pick up the wagons. The wagons were loaded down with strange-looking gear. Lots of tubing and a few tanks that weren't labeled.

"This looks serious," said Jamie. "Why are they going into our building?"

"I don't know. Maybe there was... I don't know... could there be a contaminated person in there?"

"And they decided to cover it all up by saying there's a gas leak?" said Jamie. "I don't know, but crazier things have happened in the name of trying to keep everyone from panicking. They must be doing everything they can to keep the city from turning into chaos."

Jamie and Mia watched as the four suited individuals made their way through the front doors of the apartment building. It seemed that all the residents had made their way out. The crowd parted, giving the contamination unit a very wide berth.

The crowd was starting to grow somewhat restless. With the arrival of the two Sprinter vans, it seemed that the possibility of a gas leak was less and less likely to the majority of the apartment residents.

Everyone was muttering quietly. There were hushed

conversations, with people glancing around them to see if they'd been overheard. The overall feeling was one of anxiety, fear, and deep suspicion.

"There's nothing on the news about it," said Mia, her face glued once again to her phone. "But there's a discussion on Twitter about this building. There's a hashtag for it."

"Really? What are people saying?

Before Mia could answer, a commotion erupted from the crowd. People started pointing, off towards the street.

Jamie turned to look to see three school buses driving up. The first one pulled up to the curb and stopped.

The school buses were empty. Jamie could see into the first one. The driver looked like a cop, wearing the same cheap mask that the other cops wore.

"Are they taking us somewhere?" said Mia, her voice full of fear.

"All right, everyone," the cop on the megaphone was saying. "If you would make your way to the nearest bus. We're taking you to a shelter."

"A shelter?" said Mia.

The cop then kept repeating the same phrase, and people started jostling into position, lining up for the three school buses that had now pulled up to the curbs.

There was nothing provided in the way of explanation as to why they had to leave their building, or what type of shelter they were headed to.

But the answer seemed somewhat obvious: their building had been exposed to the virus.

Jamie and Mia found themselves not yet formed into a line, standing a little off to the side.

Jamie could tell that Mia was just as scared as she was.

"What should we do?" said Jamie. It was one of the few times she ever remembered asking Mia for advice. Normally she was the practical one, the one who always knew what to do, the one that Mia came to.

"No idea," muttered Mia, her eyes moving back and forth between the lines boarding the buses and her phone. "People online are saying that they're taking us to an old school..."

"But how would they know?"

"I guess they wouldn't."

"That's the problem with that online stuff... no one really knows anything."

"Well, should we go?"

"I don't know. They're either taking us somewhere where we'll be safe... or..."

"Or...?"

"... Or we're contaminated, and they're trying to keep us away from everyone else..."

"Come on, ladies," said a cop, walking up, his hand on a thick black nightstick. "Form up. Get in line and get on the bus. It's simple. No need to make this more difficult than it has to be."

Jamie and Mia exchanged a terrified look. It seemed that they had no choice. They were getting on that bus whether they wanted to or not.

Suddenly, in her peripheral vision, Jamie spotted the sweaty man in a suit who'd come to her door. He looked even sweatier and more disheveled than he had earlier, and his eyes were wide and fixed right on Jamie.

3

MATT

Matt and Damian were sitting in traffic. They were in Matt's car, and Matt was driving. Damian, who didn't live more than a couple minutes from Matt's apartment, had begged him for a ride home, saying that his mother was supposed to pick him up, but given the circumstances, she wasn't going to be able to.

Matt, despite his best instincts, had relented and agreed to give Damian the ride.

Like the rest of the office, and like the rest of Albuquerque, Matt had gotten off early from work.

Truth be told, he'd been ready to head out on his own anyway. The news of the virus, and the implications of his calculations, had told him that he needed to do something. Either get away out of the city, or hunker down in his home and not go out.

He hadn't decided, but it turned out that he wasn't the only one who was extremely concerned.

The mayor had issued some type of emergency decree. Matt wasn't sure if everyone was required to stay home or merely strongly encouraged to do so, but the way things were looking now, it didn't seem like he would ever get back to his apartment.

His commute home was normally about twenty minutes in mild traffic. On rare occasions, there was an accident and he sat in traffic. But normally it wasn't any trouble.

But, today, everyone was headed home. The roads were a nightmare. Bumper-to-bumper traffic. He wasn't even more than a third of the way home, and he was currently wondering whether or not he should shut off his engine to save fuel. It had been at least ten minutes since he'd even moved an inch, and it was beginning to seem as if running out of gas was going to become a real risk.

"You find anything?" muttered Matt.

"Nothing new. Same shit as before."

Both Matt and Damian were glued to their phones. Damian had his in his lap, and Matt had his resting on the steering wheel.

They were both scanning the news sites, both local and national, looking for anything new.

"Still doesn't seem like they located the others..."

"No, and I don't get how that's even possible. I thought the government was tracking us all on computers and stuff... don't they supposedly know where we are all the time? Not just where we are, but where we're likely to go next, based on analyzing our past data patterns?"

"Yeah, but that's just one government agency. It's not like someone who works for the National Institute of Health is going to have access to that information... shit, my battery's almost dead."

"Just plug it in."

Matt reached down to the center console and tried to find the USB cord, but it didn't seem to be there.

"You don't have one, do you? A power cord?"

"Uh, yeah, here..."

Damian reached into his nylon satchel and pulled out a USB power cord. "Here you go," he said, his eyes already glued back on his own phone.

Matt took it. "Hey," he said. "This doesn't have an adapter."

"An adapter? I thought you had one."

"Nope."

So Matt had no way to plug his phone in. About ten more minutes, and it would be dead.

Since there might come a point later when he would need to use the phone, he switched it off to conserve the battery, and put it back in his pocket.

He wished that he'd been more prepared. Even something as simple and ordinary as a charger for the car could make a huge difference in a situation like this.

He'd always been the kind of guy who'd had an interest in "gear." He happened to find flashlights, watches, knives, and guns inherently interesting. And he'd probably spent more hours at work than he should have researching new things that he shouldn't have been spending money on.

The truth was that he'd curbed his spending dramatically in the last year, in an attempt to get completely out of debt. He didn't like the idea of owing anybody anything, so he'd sold most of the overpriced watches and knives he'd bought.

He'd kept just the essentials. A basic mechanical watch, a Seiko diver with a convenient timing bezel. Two knives. One locking folder by a decent brand. A cheap fixed-blade knife from a reliable Swiss company. And a Victorinox multi-tool, which had been an expensive present from his parents about ten years ago.

He also owned a Glock, as well as a couple of small flashlights that he powered with rechargeable AA batteries. He liked rechargeable batteries because they didn't leak as much as the standard alkaline batteries. He liked flashlights that took standard AA-size batteries, rather than something esoteric, because in a pinch, AA batteries were easier to find in a regular store.

Of course, all that gear was at his apartment. The office had a strict no-knife policy, which he'd already broken once by mistake. He'd been called into his boss's office and told quite severely that he'd be let go if he broke the "no weapons" policy once more.

Since Matt couldn't afford to lose his job, he'd had to swallow his sense of practicality and leave the knives at home.

He'd been meaning, for quite a while, to put some kind of a car kit together. But he hadn't wanted to spend the money buying anything new again, and somehow he just hadn't gotten around to it.

So all he had with him was his almost-dead cell phone and the small flashlight that never left his pocket. It put out about 15 lumens, which was enough to see at night, although not very far.

But who knew how useful the flashlight would be. Matt couldn't remember the last time he'd replaced or charged the battery, and for all he knew, he had less than half an hour of light left.

"Hey," said Damian. "Check that out."

"What?"

"Up there. That red car."

The traffic was still bumper to bumper. Still completely stopped.

The red car was an SUV. Some kind of late '90s Jeep, by the looks of it. It was four cars in front of them.

Looking through the other cars, Matt could see that there was some kind of commotion going on inside the red Jeep.

"What are they doing?"

"Looks like a dance party," said Damian.

It definitely wasn't a dance party. But it was hard to make out exactly what was happening. The Jeep's rear window was tinted just enough to make it difficult to really see clearly.

"Are they fighting?"

"Kind of looks like it."

There were at least two bodies moving around rapidly. Maybe three. Hard to say.

Limbs were flailing around. Arms and legs.

Suddenly, one of the rear doors of the Jeep flew open.

A man fell out of the Jeep. His limbs flailed as he fell.

Because of the angle, Matt had a clear look at the man, who fell right on his head.

"What the...?" muttered Damian. "Did they just throw him out?"

The Jeep door was pulled shut by someone inside the Jeep, hard enough that it slammed audibly.

The man who'd been thrown from the Jeep lay there on the ground.

But he didn't lie still. His arms and legs kept moving in a fast-paced jittery kind of way.

"Something's going on with that guy," said Damian unhelpfully.

There was blood on the man's head. And at first, Matt assumed it was blood from an injury sustained in the fall.

But as the seconds passed, and as the man kept flailing, Matt began to see that the blood was actually coming from the man's mouth and nose. And it seemed that he'd hit the back of his head on the road when he'd fallen.

"Something's wrong with that guy," said Matt. "Come on, we've got to help him. He could be having a seizure."

Matt's hand was already on the door handle before Damian responded.

"Help him? Are you kidding me?"

Something about the way Damian said it gave Matt pause, and he didn't open the door.

"Why not? Why shouldn't we help him?"

"Have you forgotten what's going on? Have you forgotten why we're stuck here in traffic? Well, I haven't. I haven't just been messing around on my phone. I've been reading the symptoms of this virus... Hemorrhaging... that means blood coming out of the orifices..."

"Oh, shit," muttered Matt, as the realization that Damian was right sunk in. "So that means that he could..."

"Be contaminated. Exactly. My guess is that's why they threw him out. He started experiencing symptoms, the other people in the car realized what was going on and decided to protect themselves."

"But it wouldn't have done any good," said Matt. "They'd already be contaminated. That's what they're saying, right? That there's a two-day "silent" period in which the virus is highly contagious but shows no signs."

"That's what they're still saying online, yeah," said Damian.

"This isn't good," said Matt.

It was a huge understatement.

Matt took his hand off the door handle, and instead he hit the button that locked all the doors at once.

Next, Matt flipped the lever over that controlled whether or not the cabin air would receive fresh air from the outside or recirculate. "I hope this control actually works," said Matt.

"What, you think it's contagious from back here? We're like four cars back..."

"No idea," said Matt. "But I don't want to take any chances."

Meanwhile, Matt couldn't take his eyes off the man who was lying on the ground. He hadn't stopped moving his arms and legs, and in fact his flailing had only grown more intense and quick.

It really did look like the man was having some kind of seizure. Except for the blood that didn't stop coming from his nose and mouth. And possibly his ears as well. Matt couldn't tell.

"Do you think we're OK?" said Matt.

"What do you mean? Whether or not we could get contaminated by that guy?"

"That, but also... what if we're already contaminated and we don't know it... what if someone in the office went to get coffee before work and brushed up against someone who'd been on that plane from Beijing?"

"Yup," said Damian. "And in that case we'd be screwed."

Matt kept waiting for Damian to say more, but he remained silent.

"So that's your answer? That we'd be screwed?"

"Well, but... yeah... hear me out... we're not going to do anything different, are we? We've still got to try to make it."

"You mean try to survive?"

"Exactly."

"Hey," said Matt. "Check it out. The guy's getting up."

The man on the ground had stopped flopping around. And, in fact, he was getting to his feet. He managed to stand up, albeit very shakily.

"Maybe he's OK after all," said Damian. "Yeah, you know what? I bet we got all worked up about this virus. I bet it's something else entirely." Damian gave a shallow, unconvincing little laugh. It was as if he really didn't want to believe the reality of the virus.

Then the man turned around so that Matt and Damian had a full-on view of his face.

It was a horrific sight.

There was blood everywhere. Blood flowing freely from his nose, some of it getting into his mouth, from which blood was coming as well.

Blood was indeed coming from his ears. Quite freely.

His eyes were bulging out, protruding from their sockets.

His face looked somehow very gaunt, as if he were a man who'd lost too much weight too quickly, as a result of some incredible physical or emotional stress.

"Shit..." muttered Damian, his voice trailing off into nothing.

Matt's heart had started to pound again, and it felt like his body was on the verge of breaking into a cold sweat.

Hearing about the terrifying potential of the virus was one thing. Thinking about it was one thing.

Seeing its effects were quite another.

The contaminated man took a single, shaking step forward. His arms were at his sides, shaking, and it seemed as if he was trying to keep his balance.

"He's coming this way," said Damian. "This isn't good, Matt. What do we do?"

Matt said nothing. He was thinking. Thinking through possibilities.

The man took another shaky step.

The car immediately in front of Matt's car suddenly turned on. The driver was apparently terrified of the approaching man, and wanted to do anything he could to get out of the way.

"There's nowhere for him to go," said Damian. "What does he think he's doing?"

It was a mid-sized standard sort of SUV. Blue in color. One of those SUVs that looked like it might not actually be built on a truck chassis.

"He's backing up," said Matt.

The SUV started to inch backwards. But there were only a couple inches between the SUV and Matt's car.

Next thing they knew, the SUV suddenly jerked backwards.

It slammed into Matt's car, making his head jerk forward.

"What the...?"

The SUV now jerked forward, slamming into the car in front of it.

Apparently the driver's plan was to smash his way out.

But no matter how much he smashed into Matt's car, or any others, he wasn't getting out.

It was bumper to bumper. There was simply no room to drive.

The sidewalk was a narrow little affair, and there was no shoulder. The lane with the oncoming traffic was bumper to bumper as well. There was no way an emergency vehicle could make its way through, and there was definitely no room for anyone who wanted to make a break for it.

If Matt wanted to get out of there, he was going to have to do it on foot, leaving his car behind.

"This isn't good," Damian was saying, his voice rising. He was getting more and more upset. "This guy's nuts..."

Once again, the SUV smashed backwards into Matt's car.

But for once, Matt wasn't remotely concerned about the damage to his car.

Bigger things were at stake.

The sick man hadn't stopped walking. The blood from his face hadn't stopped flowing. He was approaching the wild-driving SUV as if he didn't see it.

"What do you think?" said Matt, knowing he was about to have to make a quick decision. "What increases our risk of contamination more? Having this guy walk right next to our car... possibly spitting on the window, spitting blood on the car for all I know... or getting out now and making a run for it?"

Damian said nothing, but they exchanged a look. It was clear that neither of them really knew the answer. Damian knew so little that he didn't even bother responding.

If they'd already been contaminated without their knowledge, then it was all a moot point.

But as long as Matt still seemed to be uncontaminated, he was going to do everything he could to stay alive.

He just wished that he knew what it was that would increase his chances of survival.

The SUV in front of him slammed into his car again. This time, it pushed it backwards into the car behind them, the driver of which held down on the horn.

The contaminated man was getting closer.

Matt only had mere seconds to decide.

His heart was slamming around in his chest.

This might be the most important decision he'd ever had to make.

4

JAMIE

Jamie and Mia were sitting next to each other at the back of one of the school buses that were driving in tandem.

The last time Jamie had ridden a school bus, she'd been in elementary school, and one of the benches had been big enough to seat three kids. Now, three people to a bench seemed like a complete impossibility, as she and Mia were quite cramped for space, although neither one of them could be called anything but average-sized.

The buses were trundling slowly down roads with heavy traffic. At various intersections, Jamie looked out the window to see streets that were packed bumper-to-bumper with cars, completely unmoving.

Apparently they were headed towards a large convention center, where they'd be housed along with many others until the virus crisis was over.

"There's a hashtag now on Twitter for the Albuquerque convention center," Mia was saying. "We're not the only ones going there... not by a long shot."

"It just doesn't make any sense," said Jamie.

"What doesn't?"

"The fact that they're taking a bunch of us and putting us all together in the same place? Aren't we dealing with a super contagious, super deadly virus here? How is this going to stop contamination? If anything, it's going to make it worse. In close quarters, it's only going to take one sick person to make everyone sick. And by the time they get sick..."

"...it'll be too late," said Mia, finishing her sentence for her. "And everyone will be dead."

"Exactly."

"So what are you thinking?"

"I'm thinking that we don't want to end up at this convention center. The odds of getting sick there just seem too high."

"They're just trying to help us," said a man in front of her, turning around. He had an annoying sort of face, and eyeglasses that had slid about halfway down his nose.

Jamie completely ignored him. Instead, she kept her eyes focused on Mia, speaking only to her. "We've got to get out of here," she said. "I don't want to wind up there. It could be the end."

"You know," said Mia. "Some people are talking about that online... that it might not be a good idea to put everyone who might have been contaminated together in one place... sharing bedding and food and water..."

"And what are they doing about it?"

"Nothing. No one has even suggested not going. After all, it's what we're supposed to do."

"Well, I'm not like everyone else," said Jamie. "And in times like this, that can be a good thing."

It was true. Jamie wasn't like everyone else. They'd been telling her she was too headstrong for her own good since the first grade. She'd never paid it any attention, whether it had come from friends, teachers, or parents, and had just continued to do things the way that she'd wanted to.

"In times like these," said the man, who was turned around so much he wasn't really in his seat any longer. "It's important to listen to those in positions of authority."

This annoyed Jamie.

She turned to him. "Why don't you mind your own business?" she said.

"There's no need to speak to me like that," he said, looking far more offended than the words seem to call for.

"Like hell there isn't," said Jamie. "We're having a private conversation here. Mind your own business."

"But this concerns all of us," said the man. "We're all in this together."

"Look, buddy," said Jamie, laying on what she'd called her "scary face" in the past. "Turn around before I make things difficult for you."

Her "scary face" really did look scary.

And the thing was, it wasn't just for show. When things had gotten difficult at various times in her life, Jamie knew how to give her enemies a hard time.

The guy caught one look at her and turned right around, falling silent.

Mia giggled. "I remember when you did that to that regional manager who was giving you a hard time," she said.

"Come on. Let's figure out what to do."

"Well, what do you think?"

"I think we need to get off before we even get there."

"Why? Let's just wait and see what it looks like. You know how sometimes things seem like they're going to be worse than they really end up being."

"But this isn't like that," said Jamie. "This isn't something that we're nervous about... like a big presentation. We already know they're taking busloads of people there... My thinking is that once we get there, it's going to be too late. There are going to be guards keeping people in line. They're going to force us to enter the building and stay there. We're not going to have a choice. And that's not something I like. I like having a choice."

"So then what are our options? We can't just tell the driver we want to get off."

"Why not?" said Jamie. "It's a free country, right? It's not like we're under martial law or anything."

"Yeah, but it's a quarantine.... the whole city is on quarantine, I mean."

"Laws are still laws," said Jamie. "We can't be detained without good reason. I forget what the actual term is. Come on. Move over. I'm going to go talk to him."

"I think it might already be too late."

"Too late? What do you mean? There's still a ways to go."

"Look. That guy's gone to talk to the cop up front."

Jamie looked. Mia was right. The seat in front of her was empty, and the man that had been sitting in it was up front, speaking to the driver.

There was a cop in the seat behind the driver, who was talking animatedly with the other two.

The cop turned and looked back at Jamie.

Now normally Jamie had no issue with cops. In fact, she respected them. Without them, it seemed that the world would descend into chaos quickly.

But she wasn't naive enough to believe that everyone was good, no matter what their profession. There were always bad apples in every group.

And based on the way this cop up front met her eyes, she had a gut feeling that he was one of the bad apples.

She knew that it'd sound crazy if she tried to explain it to someone.

But she also knew that it wasn't crazy to trust her instincts. To go with her gut feelings. In fact, in the women's self-defense course that she'd taken about a year ago, they'd learned that simply following one's instincts was often more important than any actual moves.

The idea behind it was not that there was any "woo-woo" stuff going on. There wasn't anything psychic or weird about following gut instincts. Instead, the idea was that "gut feelings" were really just the brain's way of expressing its analysis of all sorts of data. The brain was constantly analyzing things like the body language of others, and sometimes it channeled the results of its analysis into "gut" feelings.

"I don't like the looks of that guy," said Mia.

The cop had a mean face. Maybe it was something about his eyebrows, or the way his eyes were set, but it was hard to imagine him ever not looking angry.

His eyes wouldn't leave Jamie's. And she didn't take her eyes off him.

Suddenly, his mean face broke out into a grin. But it wasn't a normal grin.

It was a grin that made her feel bad and scared.

"I don't like the looks of that..." muttered Mia next to her.

"We've got to get off this bus," said Jamie.

As soon as she spoke, the grinning cop stood up.

His head nearly scraped the ceiling of the school bus. Now that he was standing, it was obvious how large he was. His head and face didn't seem proportional to the rest of his gigantic body.

The driver said something that was only vaguely audible, and the grinning cop let out a little laugh.

The rest of the bus had fallen silent. Everyone was watching the cop, except for the few who had turned to look back at where the cop was looking, his gaze still never leaving Jamie.

"This isn't good," whispered Mia. "Looks like we're going to get in trouble."

"I need you to listen carefully and do what I say," said Jamie, taking charge, realizing that if she did nothing they'd end up at the convention center, likely getting infected.

It was a matter of life or death.

The law didn't matter now.

It didn't matter if he was a cop. If he was going to forcibly detain them, that was as good as a death sentence.

And Jamie would fight death with everything she had.

"Listen carefully to my instructions before you act," said Jamie. "I'll tell you when it's time to act. OK. You're going to get up. Then you're going to step back, towards the front of the bus. This will let me get to the back door. I'm going to open it, and then we're going to jump out."

"Are you nuts? The bus is moving. We're going to get hurt... that's a big drop down to the ground..."

"It's just like when we were kids," said Jamie. "Didn't you ever ride the bus?"

"Of course."

"Remember the fire drills we did? We'd have to jump off the back of the bus."

"Yeah, but there was always someone helping us."

Jamie knew that she might start to get frustrated with Mia. But she also knew that her frustration wasn't going to help her accomplish anything.

So instead of reprimanding Mia, she decided to try a different tactic.

"There's nothing to worry about, Mia," she said in her

most soothing voice. It was hard to speak this way, since the cop was getting closer by the second as he strode down the narrow aisle of the school bus. And when Jamie glanced over, the cop was reaching for something at his side. Either a gun or a nightstick or a taser. Maybe cuffs.

No matter what he was reaching for, it meant that somehow Jamie was going to be physically restrained. Physically trapped and taken to a place where she was convinced that she'd die.

"I'm going to jump out first, Mia," said Jamie. "And I'm going to be there for you. You're going to have to trust me on this one. When the bus driver was there for you as a kid, well, I'm going to be doing the same exact thing..."

She tried to speak soothingly. There wasn't much time. Everything hinged on convincing Mia. If Mia froze up, there'd be no escaping.

What Jamie didn't mention was that the bus would be moving, and that the impact from the jump off a moving bus would be far greater than if it had been stationary.

"Plus, you're not a kid now... it looked like a huge leap when you were a little kid. But now you're an adult... it's not going to be that bad. OK, you understand everything I said?"

Mia nodded silently. But she looked worried and hesitant.

"OK. Time to roll. Time to move. Come on."

Mia just looked at her.

Jamie gave Mia a forceful shove. "Come on," she hissed.

Now everyone in the bus was looking at them.

The cop was closer.

Mia stood up jerkily, then stepped forward towards the cop, giving Jamie room to maneuver.

Jamie stood up, grabbing hold of the tops of the bench-style seatbacks to pull herself up more forcefully.

Behind them was the emergency exit. And there was that big red handle that she expected.

There was a warning sign that she ignored. No time to read it.

She didn't bother looking to see where the cop was. Speed was what was important now. She couldn't let anything slow her down.

Jamie grabbed the handle and pulled.

At first, nothing happened.

Was it stuck?

No, she just needed to pull harder.

She positioned her body so that she could really use all her weight to her advantage. Not that she was heavy, but her body weight was enough.

An alarm sounded, but it was barely audible over the rumbling of the bus engine and the moving of the shocks on the road.

A weak red light began flashing somewhere off in the periphery of her vision. It was hardly what you would call a proper warning light. Just nothing, really.

Jamie pushed against the door, and it swung open, revealing a gaping chasm of nothing behind the school bus.

She stood there on the edge.

She didn't turn around. She knew she just had to jump.

She just had to do it.

The cop had been close enough already. If Jamie delayed too long, he'd catch Mia. Put her in cuffs. Or whatever he was going to do.

And then what? Jamie would be responsible for her friend being carted off to somewhere where she'd likely be infected. She'd be responsible for her friend's death.

She couldn't have that on her conscience.

But she also didn't want to jump.

The bus was going faster now. And the pavement seemed to be rushing behind the bus.

She'd thought it'd be easy to do. To jump.

But it wasn't.

She couldn't even tell herself that it was all mental, that it'd be alright, because she really had no idea if that was the case.

For all she knew, she might break a bone when landing. People had broken bones doing a lot less. And their necks, as well.

Whatever.

If there was anything that Jamie was good at, it was making herself do stuff she didn't want to do. It was how she'd been successful in her studies and her job.

She didn't count it off.

She just did it.

She jumped without thinking about it for another moment.

The seconds were long as she fell to the ground.

She landed, her knees buckling under her, taking more of the shock.

She felt the impact in her feet and her shins, as well as her knees.

But she didn't stay upright. Instead, because of the speed of the bus, it felt as if she was falling backwards.

She still had momentum, and she lost her balance and tumbled into the ground, splaying out on her side.

A car horn blared. Then a second one.

Someone was holding onto the horn.

There was pain in her thigh. Her work pants were torn, and there was a large road rash across her skin. A decent amount of blood. But it wasn't freely bleeding.

She scrambled to her feet, not wasting any time.

A sedan skidded to a stop about a foot away from her. The driver had his windows up, but he was clearly screaming something at her from inside the vehicle. He slammed on the horn, which blared loudly.

Jamie ignored him and turned around.

The bus was rapidly leaving her behind.

From where she stood, Jamie could see Mia perched on the edge.

She couldn't see the cop behind her.

Mia looked like she wasn't going to do it, like she wasn't going to jump. If she was going to do it, she would have done it by now.

"Come on!" shouted Jamie. "Jump!"

Mia had a terrified look on her face.

Ignoring the pain in her leg, Jamie started running after the bus, waving her hands. She needed to get Mia to jump.

She knew Mia well. She knew that Mia wasn't always good at getting things done. After all, they'd been roommates now for a year, and there'd been plenty of times when if Mia had let something like the dishes go undone for too long, then they'd never get done.

"Jump," she shouted again.

Suddenly, the cop appeared behind Mia.

Jamie was running fast now, her arms pumping at her sides to keep up with the bus. But it was still getting away from her.

The cop's hands appeared on Mia's shoulders, grabbing her. Jamie could see his big mean face framed behind her, over her shoulder.

Jamie shouted again.

Mia's look of terror turned more severe as she spun to see who had grabbed her.

Then she did it.

She jumped.

Or she tried to.

What happened instead was that she launched herself forward, but the cop managed to hold onto her with one massive hand caught under her armpit like a hook.

Mia wasn't large, and she looked like a doll as she dangled out the back of the open bus emergency exit. Her hips and legs banged against the metal below the doorway.

Mia yelped in pain.

Jamie kept running, trying to keep up.

Mia seemed to hang there forever, suspended in the air. It seemed as if the cop was too strong, as if he would simply hang on to her, never letting her go. It seemed as if he might just pull her up back into the bus.

She had to fall. She had to somehow wiggle free.

And she did.

It seemed to take forever, but she squirmed like a wild animal, her hands moving wildly, fighting back.

Then it happened. Mia was free. She fell.

The fall was fast.

She hit the pavement hard.

The next thing Jamie knew, the bus was speeding up even more, pulling away.

And Jamie had caught up to Mia, who was lying on the ground, groaning in pain.

Jamie stood there over her, protecting her from the traffic.

Horns blared. Vehicles rushed by them.

Mia's legs were at funny angles. It seemed as if she was in no position to move herself.

Jamie reached down and did what seemed impossible. She grabbed Mia with both hands and lifted her up.

Mia was by no means large.

But it was still quite a feat for Jamie.

Jamie had been meaning to start exercising again for months now. But somehow, with work, with groceries, with everyday life getting in the way, it had never happened.

Her muscles burned as she held onto Mia and walked across the road.

The traffic didn't stop for them. It just went around them.

Horns blared. People screamed out of windows.

It was all a blur.

A painful blur.

When she finally got the roadside, she didn't think she could take one more step.

She practically collapsed, but instead managed to set Mia down somewhat heavily and jerkily.

Jamie collapsed to the ground, breathing heavily. Her muscles burned. She didn't know if Mia would be able to walk.

But they were safe for now. They weren't going to be taken to the convention center. They weren't going to be infected. At least not yet. Not if they could help it.

The bus was already far off in the distance. It hadn't stopped. Jamie and Mia evidently weren't worth it to the driver and the cop.

Good.

But now the reality was settling in.

Jamie and Mia were on their own.

"You OK, Mia?"

"I'm OK. We got off."

"Yup. We made it. I cant believe you got away from that cop."

"Me neither. Thanks for carrying me."

"Sure."

"I just have one question."

"What's that?"

"What are we going to do now?"

The question really sank in.

What *were* they going to do now?

Where were they going to go?

If the convention center was dangerous because it had too many people, then what place in the city of Albuquerque wouldn't be dangerous? After all, there were people everywhere.

To stay safe, they'd have to get somewhere where there weren't any other people.

But where was that place? Where would they go?

Did they need to get out of the city? Far away?

"Can you walk, Mia?"

"I don't know yet. I'm going to try."

"OK. I'll help you. Just give me a minute. I need to rest."

As she lay there resting, the traffic streaming by noisily, Jamie's thoughts raced with plans and potential places to head to.

Matt had finally made up his mind.

He hadn't had much time.

He'd just had to make a decision.

"We're going," he said, speaking quickly and decisively. He didn't want Damian to argue with him and screw everything up. After all, there wasn't much time. "Hold onto your stuff. Open your door when I do. Then run backwards away from the rear of the car. Follow me."

Matt was in decent shape. Over the last couple years, he'd taken several small twenty-minute time segments out of his week, dedicating them to keeping himself in reasonable physical condition.

He'd never cared much about how he looked, as long as he could fit into his clothes.

Matt happened to care more about being "functionally" fit. He didn't like the idea of not being able to do things. And eventually, if his muscles deteriorated in the way that happens to a lot of people with desk jobs, he knew he'd end up old and incapable.

He hadn't liked the idea of not being capable. He wanted

to be able to take care of himself for as long as possible. It was part of his whole self-sufficiency dream.

In devising his workout plan, he'd intentionally shunned the internet, which was full of gimmicks for creating big bulky muscles that didn't do anything. Instead, he'd taken the boring, long route, heading to the local university library to read scientific papers on muscle development and strength improvement.

Eventually he'd settled on a simple program, basing it mainly on old-school strongman workouts, which seemed to be closest in line with the facts that the research papers presented.

He did sprints weekly. And the rest of the time, he trained with weights. Not actual weights bought in a store, but simply improvised things like five-gallon buckets filled with water, bags of sand, and cinder blocks that he'd tied together with chains from Home Depot. Those ideas, he had to admit, he had gotten from the internet.

He hadn't trained with the "standard" exercise movements. He'd shunned anything that worked a single muscle, like bicep curls.

Instead he'd done things like pick up the cinder blocks with one hand and walk up and down the steps.

He'd done things like hoist a sandbag high above his head, and do squats.

They were exercises that worked multiple muscle groups at the same time. Compound movements.

This is what all that training had been for.

Hopefully. Hopefully, it helped somehow.

So he knew he was up to the task of sprinting away from the car. He knew he'd be faster than Damian. He needed to make sure Damian didn't chicken out.

"You got this, Damian?" he said. "You going to follow through?"

"Yeah," said Damian, nodding his head very fast. But he looked scared. He looked like he might puke, and his eyes didn't leave the sick man who was walking towards them.

"Come on, Damian," said Matt, changing his mind and changing his plan. "You're going to go first. I'll be right behind you."

It was risky. If Damian choked and didn't run, there wouldn't be much time for Matt. He might get stuck too close to the contaminated man.

If only he had more information on how the contamination process of the virus worked. It seemed like the virus might be transmitted through the air, through the respiratory system, but that was really nothing more than a guess.

How close could he safely get to the contaminated man?

He had no idea.

For all he knew, he was actually contaminated already.

It wasn't a pleasant thought. But it was realistic. After all, all it would take is one person at the office to have somehow run into someone from that plane from Beijing. Or to just have run into someone who'd run into someone who'd run into someone from the plane.

No point in worrying about it.

The contaminated man was closer. Not far away now.

The vehicle in front of them slammed once again into Matt's car, making it rock backwards.

Horns were blaring.

They had to go.

It was time.

Matt formed his hand into a fist and slammed it hard into Damian's arm. "You got this, Damian," he said. "Now go!"

He basically screamed the words right into Damian's ear. Otherwise, his friend might just sit there and not move.

Damian moved. Matt breathed a mental sigh of relief.

Damian threw his door open and hopped out of the car.

Matt did the same. He didn't grab anything. There was nothing there that was useful to him.

The contaminated man was about ten feet away. Matt could see his face more clearly than ever before.

It was covered in blood.

The flow of blood wasn't slowing down. There was so much of it. It was completely disgusting. The sheer amount of the blood provoked a visceral response in Matt.

His body started moving as if he was about to throw up. He felt nauseous.

Damian was running. Fast. Very fast.

Matt didn't even know if he'd be able to catch up to him.

His fears about Damian's speed had been for nothing. Damian was plenty fast enough.

Matt turned on his heel, ignoring the strong urge to vomit. That was the way to deal with all the feelings. Just ignore them. Push through it.

Now Matt was running.

He was sprinting. Right next to the cars. Inches away from them.

His feet were pounding against the pavement. His arms were pumping at his sides.

His breathing was heavy and ragged.

He kept his head back, his chin tucked. He used all the techniques that he'd trained with, the ones that had become completely second nature to him.

He was catching up with Damian. Just a couple feet behind him.

Damian was coming up to an intersection.

"Take the left!" shouted Matt.

Damian made no indication that he'd heard him, but when he reached the intersection, he swerved between the cars, and made the left.

It seemed as if everyone was honking, and as if the cars were all moving, all slamming into each other. The traffic had turned into madness.

It was a relief to get onto the next street. There were no cars, except some that were parked. This street led nowhere, really. It seemed to be just a cross street.

Albuquerque was big, and Matt, while he knew his way around, certainly hadn't been everywhere.

He'd passed this street hundreds of times, but had never had reason to drive down it.

Damian was still running.

Matt had slowed his own pace after looking over his shoulder, seeing there was no one following them. The bleeding man had no chance of catching up to them. After all, he had looked as if he might collapse to the ground any moment, and he certainly wasn't going to be getting up and running.

Damian kept running and running, until he had gotten about halfway down the street.

Then he fell into a heap on someone's front lawn.

Matt caught up to him. He was exhausted. Out of breath.

Damian was breathing hard, doubled over, lying on his side.

Matt's mind was rushing almost as fast as he had been running.

Suddenly, everything seemed real. And serious.

He'd just left his car there in the middle of the road. The doors wide open. The engine on.

Not to mention all his work papers. He'd left those in the car.

The car wasn't even completely paid off yet.

But this was life or death.

It took them a full minute to catch their breath enough to really talk.

"What now?" said Damian, speaking first, breathing heavily through his words.

"Back to my place," said Matt, without thinking.

"Your place? Why?"

"We're not that far. We can walk from here."

"We should have just stayed in the car then."

"Even if it hadn't been for the risk of infection, I doubt we would have gotten there in the car inside of several hours. We'll get there faster on foot."

"And then what? Hole up in your place? I should check on my mom..."

"My apartment is in a building," said Matt. "A big building. One of those complexes. I don't think it's going to be a good place to lie low. Too many neighbors. Not enough ways out."

"Then why go there?"

"I've got some gear."

"Like a gun?"

"Not 'like' a gun. A gun."

"I didn't know you were like that."

"You didn't know I was practical?"

"No, I just..."

"Forget it. It doesn't matter. But what does matter is that I'm going to feel a lot better when I have a gun in my hand."

"Come on. Do you really need a gun? I mean, we're trying to avoid a virus here. Not rob a bank."

"Is that what you think guns are for? Robbing banks?"

"I don't know," said Damian, sounding stupid.

"There's going to be a lot more to worry about than just avoiding the virus," said Matt. "What do you think is going to happen if a large percentage of the population dies?"

"I don't know."

"It's going to be chaos, that's what," said Matt. "And when there's chaos, there's violence. People aren't going to be able to help themselves. If enough people die, society isn't going to be able to hold itself together. It's going to break down. The rules are going to break down. And then people are going to go wild. Those who've been hemmed in by the rules, they're going to go wild. So that's why I want the gun."

"How do you know all this? Where's the proof."

"I don't need proof. It's just common sense. Stuff I've always known. Just kind of figured it out. What are you doing?"

"Checking my phone."

"Right now? Come on, we've got to get a move on it."

"Just a second. I think I found something here."

"What site are you on?"

"Twitter."

Matt scoffed. "Come on. Go to a real site. You're not going to find anything on there. That's just social media junk. Can't people get off that crap during something serious? I mean, really, a virus outbreak and you've got to check Twitter? This isn't a joke..."

"There's something good here, though."

"What?"

"There's some hashtag... something about enlarged veins. Hang on..."

"We don't have time for this," said Matt, standing up. He was still panting, but he knew it was time to go.

"Wait... there's a link..."

"Come on, Damian."

Damian stood up and Matt started walking down the street. His own cell phone was still off and inside his pocket. He didn't need to use it to get home. He knew the way. It was simple enough.

"You coming?"

"Yeah," muttered Damian, jogging to catch up with him, his eyes still glued to his cell phone.

"You're going to drain the battery on that thing."

"I know, I know, but listen... they're saying that there's actually a sign..."

"A sign of what?"

"A sign that you're infected."

That got Matt's attention. To say that it had been on his mind would be an understatement.

"What do they say?"

"Those infected have enlarged veins... in the hands, fore-arms, in particular. Also, the neck, it looks like... maybe the forehead... I'm not sure... I'm not sure that they're sure"

"But where's this from? What's the source?"

"I saw it on Twitter... but wait... it's on every news outlet."

"Seriously?"

"Yeah. All the main sites. There's even something on the CDC... it says that's the Center for Disease Control."

"I know what the CDC is," snapped Matt, grabbing the phone from Damian. "Here, let me see that."

He didn't really care about being rude. After all, Damian didn't have the best reputation at the office for being prudent about things. And sometimes he had been known to get quite carried away on far-fetched tangents, rather than staying rooted in reality.

Matt needed to check it out for himself.

But it seemed that Damian's obsessive phone and social media habit had actually paid off, because it seemed as if it was true.

Matt made sure to check the URL in the browser. He knew that it was quite possible to set up fake news sites, and even fake CDC sites. The link would simply take the Twitter user to a fake site that looked identical to the real one.

But, no, these were the real sites. Unless the CDC and all the major news sites had been hacked, the news seemed legitimate.

Before he even handed the phone back to Damian, Matt looked down at the veins in his hand.

He breathed a sigh of relief. They looked a little large, but they always did. They certainly didn't look anything like the picture that the CDC page showed, with someone's veins at least three times as large as normal.

"You good?" said Damian.

Matt knew what he meant. He meant the veins.

"Yeah, I'm good. Clean. What about you?"

"Me too."

"Let me see."

There was a long pause.

It probably did seem like a weird thing to ask. It probably did seem as if he didn't trust him.

And he didn't.

He didn't really trust Damian. He'd felt that way all along, ever since the first day he'd met him at work, but now he actually realized it.

"You don't trust me?" Damian sounded hurt.

"This isn't the kind of thing you can trust someone on... Here, look at mine."

They were stopped in the middle of the empty street. Matt held out the back of his hand for Damian to examine.

Then Damian did the same.

His veins looked normal. They were dilated even less than Matt's.

Matt just nodded at Damian, turned, and then started walking again.

Damian caught up to him, matching his quick pace, walking at his side.

"It's good we know about the veins," said Damian. "Now we know who to avoid."

"Yeah. Sometimes you can't see veins, though," said Matt. "Better be on the safe side."

"What does that mean?"

"Just avoid everyone."

"Everyone? How are we going to do that."

"I'm still working on it," said Matt, pointing to his head, indicating that he was thinking about it. "Did it say anything else about the virus? Any more information? About the vectors of contamination? About how it works?"

"No, not really. Just the stuff about the veins. I don't think you saw it, because it was at the bottom of the page. But they said that the veins are the result of increased nitric oxide."

"Some type of hormone or something, right?"

"I think so."

"Doesn't do us much good to know that," said Matt.

"I guess not."

As they walked, they kept up a fast enough pace that they were actually breathing hard, as if they had been lightly jogging.

"How much battery you got left on your phone?" said Matt.

"Not much. About 20 percent."

"You'd better turn it off."

"But I want to see if there's any more news."

"You can check it later."

Damian mumbled something about his mother calling him, and it didn't seem like Matt was going to be able to make him turn the phone off, so he gave up.

It didn't take long to get to Matt's apartment building. They kept to the little side city streets as much as they could.

The major thoroughfares, normally not too crowded, were all stop-and-go traffic. Cars simply weren't moving. When Matt and Damian had to take these roads for brief periods, they kept on the far side of the sidewalks, and moved as quickly as they could.

They didn't see anything quite as crazy as what had prompted them to abandon Matt's vehicle, but they could tell that people were starting to lose their patience.

Here and there, there were minor fender benders. There were people yelling at each other out of windows. There were people laying on their horns.

But, perhaps because of fear of the virus, no one seemed to want to get out of their cars.

Matt and Damian were the only people on foot, out of a vehicle. They came across no one else, all the way back to Matt's apartment.

They stood outside the apartment building, in the parking lot, which was for the most part empty.

"I guess no one managed to get back from work yet," said Matt, surveying the mostly empty parking lot.

"So what's wrong with staying here?" said Damian. "It's like abandoned. We're not going to get infected..."

"I thought you wanted to check on your mom? Her place isn't that far away, is it?"

"Yeah, I was thinking..."

"Thinking what?"

"I don't know. I was just thinking about that infected guy... blood all over his face... what if we don't make it to my mom's place? Without running into a guy like that, I mean. Anyone could be infected..."

"So you want to abandon your own mother and just stay put at my apartment? Is that it? Because you're scared."

"Uh, basically," said Damian, not meeting Matt's gaze, keeping his eyes fixed on the parking lot pavement. "I mean, I'll call her... make sure she's OK."

Matt just shook his head vaguely at Damian's attitude about his own mother. "Don't you live with her?"

"Yeah, but what's that got to do with anything? Lots of people live with their parents..."

Damian had been made fun of a little bit at work in the last few months for living with his mother, and it seemed that he'd developed an automatic and defensive verbal response to anything he perceived as an attack.

"Well, *I'm* not staying here," said Matt. "Eventually, someway or somehow, people will get home. We don't yet know how close you need to be to someone to get the virus... I'd rather be somewhere where I don't share a wall with anyone."

"Then what's the plan?"

"How about this? You wait here. I'll be right back with my stuff."

"You mean your gun?"

"Yes, my gun. At some point, you're going to be glad that I have it."

Damian nodded vaguely. "Maybe..."

"I'll meet you back here. Then we'll go to your mom's house. It's a regular house, right?"

"Yeah, pretty normal..."

"It's not a duplex, right?"

"No, it stands on its own."

"Decent-sized yard?"

"Pretty big for a city, I guess."

"OK. So we'll go there. Hole up there. OK?"

"Uh, sounds good. Not sure how my mom's going to feel about it..."

"She's met me before. She likes me. I bet she'll be fine with it. Probably be glad to have someone else around who knows how to use a gun."

Damian nodded vaguely.

Matt left him there, standing near a tree in the nearly empty parking lot.

Matt hesitated only a moment at the front door of the apartment building, then he entered.

It was deathly quiet in the carpeted corridors.

But that was normal. Almost everyone who lived in the building worked a nine-to-five job.

Matt walked through the corridors to the stairwell.

He never took the elevator, and he wasn't going to start now. So he climbed up to the third floor, and walked down the long hallway.

His apartment was at the end of the hall.

The carpet muffled his quick footsteps.

Matt was anxious to have his Glock with him once again, and he was walking fast.

Why hadn't he taken it to work with him? He'd been meaning to figure out a way to carry it concealed without it "printing" on his work clothes at all, but hadn't yet figured out how to do it. The Glock was fairly large, and current male office fashion didn't allow for a lot of loose fabric.

Still, he should have had it in his car at least. Or a bag.

He shouldn't have just left it at home, where it did him no good at all.

He'd screwed up big time and he knew it.

But he was about to fix all that.

Matt arrived at the end of the hall. He'd reached his apartment door, which was closed. Just the way he'd left it.

He had his key in his hand already, and was about to put it into the lock, when for some reason, he decided to check the doorknob first.

It was something that he remembered his mom doing every time they'd come home from being away for a good while. She'd been the nervous sort, and always seemed to expect someone with bad intentions to be waiting for them inside.

The doorknob turned.

The door wasn't locked.

But he'd definitely left it locked.

Why was his door unlocked?

He wasn't a careless person. He'd never left his door unlocked before. Just like he'd never lost his keys or his cell phone. It just wasn't part of his personality.

Matt paused for a moment, trying to figure out what to do.

The way he saw it, he didn't have any choice but to enter his apartment. He needed his Glock. As the virus took hold of the city, things were only going to get worse. People were only going to get more violent. And desperate.

And the rest of the gear wouldn't hurt.

Matt's hand turned the doorknob.

Whoever had entered his apartment might still be there. If they were, he'd have to deal with them. Without his Glock. Without anything but his bare hands and his wits.

6

JAMIE

J amie and Mia hadn't known where to go. They had felt horribly vulnerable out in the open, on the road with no vehicle. And they couldn't go back to their apartment, which was apparently contaminated.

So they'd gone to the first place that had crossed Jamie's mind: Matt's apartment.

"This is so weird," said Mia, sitting down on one of his chairs in the living room. "It's like we're breaking into to your ex's house."

"He's not my ex. We just went out on three dates."

"If he's not your ex, then why do you have his spare key? That's like *so* weird. And you didn't even tell me..."

Jamie shrugged. It was weird that she had his key. What could she say? It was one of the reasons that she'd broken it off with Matt. He'd just come on way too strong and way too fast. The way he'd been talking on that third date, it had sounded like he wanted to marry her. And when he'd given her the key, it had just been too much for her. Too much and too fast. Way too intense.

"And you didn't even give the key back? That's even weirder, in my opinion."

Jamie felt herself starting to feel defensive. "Hey," she said. "He's the one who gave it to me. Then we just didn't talk at work. He gave me the complete silent treatment. It was like I wasn't even there... what was I supposed to do? How was I supposed to get it back to him? I did what anyone would have, which was ignore the situation. It was just too weird to deal with."

Mia made a little noise of confirmation. "It's just so weird that he gave you a key..."

"Yeah, I know."

"Is he like just totally weird or something?"

"That's the thing. He doesn't seem weird any other way. Actually, he was pretty normal and nice before we started to go out... I think he just hadn't gone on a date in a little while and took the whole thing way more seriously than..."

"...than is remotely normal?" Mia finished the sentence for her.

"Basically."

"I've heard about guys like that," said Mia. "They just go nuts when it comes to dating... like they just become way too intense."

"Yeah," said Jamie, nodding. "But, hey, let's drop it for a moment, all right? There's more important stuff going on."

"I'm not even giving you a hard time, though," said Mia, her voice rising, sounding like a complaint.

"I know. But look, let's get back to reality here. What happened between me and Matt isn't going to keep us alive. I mean, what are we going to do?"

"Let's just stay here," said Mia, stretching out her long legs, throwing her arms behind her head, making herself comfortable.

"Stay here? Are you crazy?"

"Why not? I checked the fridge. There's some food. Not a lot, but there's enough stuff in the freezer... some of these frozen microwave dinners that guys are always eating... We'll just wait out all this commotion here, and then when it dies down... I've been meaning to go on a diet anyway." She patted her small, nonexistent belly, as if she was acknowledging that she needed to slim down.

"You think this is going to die down soon?" said Jamie, incredulously.

"Sure. I mean, how long could it last? The government will get it under control, right?"

Jamie made a scoffing sound.

"You don't think so? You don't trust the government or something?"

"It's not that I don't trust them," said Jamie. "It's just that I'm realistic. And a good judge of human character. The government, after all, is made up of people. It's made up of human beings who are very fallible. They make errors and they make mistakes. And this is going to be a massive problem... if the virus is as contagious as they say it is, the numbers of contaminated people are going to rise exponentially... It's going to be completely insane."

"But how do you know all that?" said Mia. "Why do you think you know more than the people on the news? They're saying that it's going to all be over within a week. Everything will calm down."

"Yeah, of course that's what they're going to say," said Jamie. "But you've got to remember that they're primarily a business. A business that makes money off advertisements. Why would they predict the end of their entire business model?"

"You're just talking like a crazy person now," said Mia,

sinking further into a more comfortable position. Her posture was so relaxed that it looked like she might fall asleep at any moment.

Jamie knew that they couldn't start arguing. It would just be counterproductive. But she also knew that she needed to come up with a plan. She needed to figure out what they'd do and where they'd go.

Maybe Mia was right in that they could stay in Matt's apartment for a little while. Maybe a few days? Maybe something would change, even if the situation didn't improve, in some way that would allow them to move somewhere else more secure.

What about Matt? Where was he? She didn't like the idea of being in his apartment if he came home.

She actually shivered at the thought of how awkward the encounter would be. What would she say?

She actually started running through things in her head that she could say if Matt showed up.

She supposed that she'd just have to tell the truth, that she and her friend were in a tight spot, fearing for their lives, and had nowhere else to go.

Or maybe she could make a joke about finally using that key he'd given her? Maybe it would alleviate some of the awkwardness, some of the tension.

Or maybe it wouldn't?

"What are you doing?" said Mia, sleepily. "You're going into his bedroom?"

Jamie didn't answer.

But it was true. She was entering Matt's bedroom.

It was the first time she'd been in there. And she was only going in because it seemed important to her to scope out the entire apartment.

Maybe there'd be something useful in there.

And just for peace of mind, it was nice to know that the whole place was empty.

Well, there was no one in the room.

The bedroom was actually quite boring. It was neat and tidy. She'd always heard that most single guys had horribly messy bedrooms.

But that wasn't the case with Matt. Everything seemed to be in its proper place.

Not that there was really that much to have to worry about putting away.

The bedroom really was just the bed, a bureau, a nightstand, and a closet.

There wasn't much of interest in the nightstand drawer. Some Chapstick and a small flashlight. That was about it, along with a couple of pens and a small notebook.

In the bureau, there were really just clothes.

In the closet, more clothes. Boring clothes, too. The kind of stuff that Matt wore to work. Just plain blue button-down shirts and khaki pants.

But what was that, there in the corner of the closet, covered by a thin piece of fabric?

She pulled the fabric away to reveal a safe.

She bent down to examine it. It was an old-fashioned combination safe. It wasn't digital. Instead it had the big dial with a lot of numbers on it.

What did he have in that safe?

A gun. It was probably a gun.

He didn't really seem like the gun-owning type. He'd never mentioned it.

But that didn't really mean anything.

Jamie suddenly found herself wishing that she had a gun. She'd actually grown up with guns, back in Philadelphia. Her father had taken her and her sister to the range more than a few times. He'd even had a family friend, a well-known firearms instructor in the area, take her and her sister shooting, showing them how to properly use a firearm.

So she'd shot rifles, shotguns, and some smaller pistols. She'd tried shooting her dad's .45, but the kickback had been too much for her to feel comfortable with. At least, back then.

It had been almost a decade since she'd moved away from Pennsylvania and her parents. And almost just as long since she'd fired a gun.

But she sure would have liked to have one with her now.

She glanced at the safe one more time, wondering again if it really contained a gun, and then turned around and left the bedroom. She headed towards the kitchen, deciding that it'd be valuable to take stock of exactly how much food there was, before they decided whether or not they were going to stay there and if so, for how long.

Suddenly, Mia screamed out.

"What is it?"

Jamie made it into the room in a flash.

Mia had sat bolt upright. She was staring at the entrance.

Jamie turned, and saw someone standing there. A man. Holding a lamp high above his head in a threatening way, as if he was ready to strike someone with it.

"What are you doing here?" he said.

He kept his distance, staying as far away from Mia and Jamie as he could.

Suddenly, Jamie realized who it was. The situation was so startling she hadn't realized that the man was Matt. Matt from work. Matt, her coworker. Matt, who she'd dated and never spoken to again. Matt whose apartment she'd broken into.

She almost asked him what he was doing there before she realized it made complete sense that he was here. It was his apartment after all.

Then her mind started racing, trying to figure out how she could explain what she and her friend were doing there.

She felt overcome with embarrassment. Her face started to get bright red.

It had been a lot to go through, not speaking to him at work. And now? She'd broken into his apartment. That was 'crazy ex-girlfriend' behavior. But she'd never even been his girlfriend.

"Let me see your veins," he said, still across the room.

"My veins?" said Jamie.

"This was all her idea," said Mia. "I didn't even want to break in. But she said it'd be OK. She said that you gave her a key, after all, and all that..."

"Mia!" hissed Jamie.

"Show me your veins!" said Matt, raising his voice. He sounded mad.

"What are you talking about?"

"You don't know?"

"Know what?" Jamie took a step forward towards Matt. "Matt, I know this is really weird... me breaking into your apartment, but I can explain it all..."

"Stay back!" shouted Matt, raising the lamp higher into the air. "The veins on the back of your hand. Hold up your hands so I can see the back of them... both of you."

Fear shot through Jamie and she froze in place. This didn't seem like Matt. He'd always seemed calm.

Jamie glanced over at Mia. They exchanged a look that more or less said, 'I don't know what this is about, but we'd better do what he says. He seems to have a good reason for wanting to do this.'

Only when both Jamie and Mia had held up their hands, and Matt was peering at them, did it occur to Jamie that this must have something to with the do virus.

"Your necks. Let me see your necks," said Matt. He seemed a little more relaxed. But only just a little bit.

"Our necks?"

"Crane them out. Let me see the sides... the veins..."

"This is nuts," said Mia, already holding her neck out as best she could.

Jamie did the same.

"Is that a sign of the virus or something?" said Jamie.

"I thought you said you hadn't heard about it?" said Matt, taking a couple steps towards them, lowering the lamp as he did so.

"I hadn't. But I just figured it out, I guess. What were you looking for?"

"Apparently infected people have dilated veins in their hands and necks," said Matt.

"It's true," said Mia, her eyes glued to her phone, her thumb scrolling across its touch screen. "Looks like they finally figured out how to tell if someone's been contaminated... they're still saying that the virus is 'silent' for two days before it starts to kill the host..."

"That's kind of a relief," said Jamie.

Matt was walking slowly towards her. "So," he was saying. "What are you doing in my apartment?"

Jamie realized it was the first time they'd talked since their last date. Still, she had the presence of mind to say loudly. "Stop!"

"Stop?"

"Stop where you are. Show me your hands."

Various expressions seemed to run across Matt's face.

Then, after a moment, he said, "Makes sense."

He stayed where he was, put the lamp down, and held up his hands so that Jamie and Mia could clearly see the backs of them. Then he craned his neck forward.

"He looks clean," said Jamie.

"Sorry about her," muttered Mia. "She's a little, you know... overly cautious."

Jamie felt the anger rising in her. She wasn't about to apologize for something like that.

"There's nothing to apologize for," said Matt. "If there ever were a time to be overly cautious, it's now."

It was a strange feeling, having Matt agree with her. And the strangeness of the situation started to sink in.

But before she could have much time to reflect on it, and before Matt could say anything else, there was a knock at the door.

Jamie felt her heart immediately start to beat faster and harder. Mia sat bolt upright, her eyes wide and fixed on the door rather than her cell phone.

"Don't worry," said Matt. "It's probably just Damian. My buddy. You know? From the office."

Jamie breathed a sigh of relief.

"He was waiting for me in the parking lot," said Matt, turning around and taking a step towards the door.

"Wait!" said Jamie. "Ask who it is."

"Good call..." said Matt. Then calling out in a louder voice, he said, "Who is it?"

"Your neighbor!" The voice was male, but it definitely wasn't Damian's.

Jamie didn't know Damian that well, but she knew his voice. It had always sounded a little funny to her, a little cartoonish, maybe a little bit effeminate.

The voice on the other side of the door, on the other hand, sounded intensely masculine.

Matt didn't take another step forward. Instead, he grabbed the lamp.

Jamie got the sense that Matt didn't recognize the voice as belonging to one of his neighbors.

Her heart was pounding her chest as she stared at the door, as if it might burst open at any moment.

In her estimation, there were two dangers.

One, the guy on the other side of the door could be violent. He could want something, and he could be willing to take it by force.

Two, he could be infected with the virus. This was by far the most serious threat. He didn't even have to do anything to kill them all.

7

DAMIAN

Matt seemed to be taking forever in his apartment, and Damian was starting to wish that he'd gone in with him.

Damian was tired from all the running and walking. Unlike Matt, he wasn't used to doing much physical activity aside from walking around the office.

Back in high school, he'd been a cross-country runner. He'd kept it up in college a little bit, taking some pleasure in long runs on the weekend. But he'd done those mostly so that he had something to do other than studying.

When he'd joined the workforce was when he'd really fallen off the wagon when it came to exercising. And consequently, he'd put on a decent-sized paunch. Overall, he was relatively skinny, but he definitely wasn't in shape, in any sense of the word.

In order to rest, Damian had found a small concrete bumper to sit down on. He'd pulled out his phone, despite the low battery, and was scrolling through his various social media feeds.

People all over the country were confirming that the dilated or enlarged veins were the sign of contamination.

There were also reports that asymptomatic people were starting to show symptoms. The reports hadn't yet showed up on the official news sites, but they were all over social media. And they seemed to be real, because the symptoms that people were describing exactly matched the man with blood on his face that he and Matt had seen in the road.

There were even a few videos. Damian clicked on one, and it started playing.

The video on his small cell phone screen showed a woman in her late fifties walking along the sidewalk. There was so much blood on her face that it was hard to tell which orifice it was coming from. The blood was actually dripping off her face onto the sidewalk, leaving a trail behind her as she walked.

Shit. This was serious stuff. People were already showing symptoms and dying. The comments for the video said that the woman had died half an hour later in a pool of her own blood.

Damian's phone started ringing. For several seconds, he didn't notice, because he was so absorbed in reading the comments of the terrified people in the video.

Then he realized that he was getting a call, and he shifted his attention to the box on the screen that displayed who was calling.

It read, "Mom."

He sighed and swiped to answer the phone.

"Hey, mom," he said.

His mom was the sort of person who scared a lot of people. She was what some called a "tough cookie." For a long time, Damian hadn't exactly understood what people had meant, even though he'd heard a lot of people talk about his mom all the way through his childhood. It wasn't until he was an adult that he understood.

She just didn't take shit from anyone.

And she wasn't happy about him living with her. In fact, the only reason that she allowed it, for a short time, was that Damian's father had just passed away recently.

His parents had been divorced since he was two years old, but he'd still seen his father on a regular basis, and the loss of him had had a tremendous impact on Damian.

"I thought you were getting a ride home from your friend," she said. "There's all kinds of crazy stuff on the news. Are you OK?"

"Yeah, I'm OK. Are you?"

"I'm fine."

"No one's bothering you? Giving you a hard time?"

"Of course not. What are you talking about? It's just me. And if someone tries to mess with me, they're going to have to answer to me. When are you getting here?"

"The whole thing's a long story," said Damian. "Basically the traffic was too bad and we had to walk..." Damian didn't want her to worry, so he didn't tell her everything else that had happened.

"Who? You and your work friend?"

"Yeah, Matt. Is it OK if he comes over too? He doesn't have anywhere else to go, and his apartment isn't OK to stay in."

"I suppose so. Just get here as soon as you can. Things on the news are just getting crazier..."

"Hey, buddy!" someone was shouting from across the parking lot.

Damian looked up. There were two young guys, both about twenty years old.

He couldn't make out their features, except that their

faces seemed unusually pale, as if they hadn't spent much time outdoors. In Albuquerque where the sun was strong, their paleness really stood out.

They looked like the kind of guys that he wouldn't want to run into in an alley late at night.

"Yeah, you!" shouted the other one, clearly pointing at Damian.

Damian turned around and, seeing no one else there, realized that they were talking to him. And him alone.

"Mom, I've got to go."

"What's going on? I heard someone shouting."

"Nothing. I'll see you soon. Don't worry."

"But..."

Damian knew that he couldn't concentrate on this new threat of the two young men while also trying to keep his Mom calmed down. So he just hung up the phone, and put it back into his pocket.

He stood up slowly, facing the two young men.

They were walking towards him now. Quickly. They walked side-by-side, with their arms and legs moving fast.

Damian looked around. The parking lot was still deserted. And the street was too. All the traffic must have been concentrated on the larger roads. This was just a road that went nowhere.

What should he do?

And where was Matt? What was taking him so long?

"Hey!" One of the guys was pointing his finger at Damian as he walked forward. He had long, greasy hair.

The closer the guys got, the more muscular they looked.

One of the men had something stuck into his waistband. It was obscured by his shirt, but Damian had the idea that it was probably a weapon of some sort.

Damian wanted to run into Matt's apartment building.

Run into Matt's apartment. He knew which one it was, since he'd been there once before for an office poker game.

But the guys were cutting across the parking lot in such a way that blocked him from accessing the building.

The guys were close now. Only a few feet away.

Anger was etched all over their faces.

Damian looked pointedly at their necks, trying to see if they were infected or not.

Their veins didn't look enlarged, but it was a little hard to tell.

"How can I help you gentlemen?" said Damian. The word came out unnaturally. It felt like something that someone might say in a movie, not something that he'd say in real life.

"You know what you did!"

The one guy got really close to Damian, not lowering his outstretched hand or his finger. He put his finger right in Damian's face, to the point where it actually touched Damian's nose.

"I'm sorry," said Damian. "I really don't know what..."

"Enough!" screamed the guy. "You can't pull this kind of stuff with us. Not again. Not after last time. Where's the money?"

"I think this is a classic case of mistaken identity," said Damian.

That's when the punch landed.

Damian didn't even see the swing.

But he definitely felt the punch.

His vision seemed to shake. He felt like he was losing his balance as the world seemed to tilt in front of him.

It seemed as if he might fall, simply collapse to the ground.

He managed to stay upright.

But not for long.

He actually saw the second punch coming in. A right hook. Aimed right at his temple.

He raised both his hands, thinking that he'd somehow block the punch.

But the punch was too fast. Too powerful. It blew past his hands.

Damian was too weak.

The punch hit him in the temple.

His vision went funny, and he collapsed to the ground, crumpling to the parking lot pavement.

"Check his pockets," said a voice above him. "I know he's got it."

Got what? thought Damian.

Whatever it was that they were looking for, he knew he didn't have it, and he worried about what they'd do when they discovered that.

8

MATT

There wasn't time to discuss why Jamie and the other woman were in his apartment.

"Do you recognize the voice?" whispered Jamie.

Matt shook his head.

It was the truth. He didn't recognize the voice. And not only that, but the voice didn't sound like one of his neighbors.

He wasn't exactly on a first-name basis with his neighbors. It was the kind of apartment building where people tended to mind their own business and stay to themselves. Even in New Mexico, which was often considered a little friendlier than the rest of the country, there were plenty of apartment buildings like this. More so now that the city was growing and more outsiders like himself were moving in daily.

Matt did, however, know what his neighbors looked like. Most of them, at least. And this big deep burly voice didn't match the image that he had in his head of any of them.

"What are you going to do?" whispered the woman that he didn't know.

"Hey, open up," came the male voice from the other side of the door.

"Hang on," yelled out Matt, trying to stall for time, not knowing what to do.

If he opened the door, he might be attacked.

But even worse than that, he might simply be infected by the virus.

As he stood there, his mind racing, he suddenly realized the absurdity of the situation.

Why didn't he just tell the stranger to go away, that he wasn't going to open the door for risk of the virus? What was he trying to do, win an award for politeness?

And that way, if the neighbor refused and tried to break in, at least Matt would know what he was working with.

"I'm not going to open the door," called out Matt, not taking another step forward, and thanking himself for having the presence of mind to lock the door behind him when he'd entered the apartment. "You might be infected."

"Fair enough," came the voice. "Just wanted to let you know that they're saying they're going to evacuate the building..."

"Evacuate the building?" called out Matt.

But the voice didn't come again. The man was gone.

"That's what they did to my building," said Jamie. And then she told him how she and her roommate, Mia, who she introduced briefly in mid-sentence, had jumped off a bus on their way to some kind of holding center.

Matt had to admit that Jamie had probably done the right thing. "Sounds like you made the right call," he said. "Now let's not let the same thing happen to us. Come on, we've got to get out of here."

Necessity was dictating that he ignore the strangeness of Jamie breaking into his apartment.

But in a way, he was glad for that. He didn't want to have to go over how he'd given her a key. Looking back on it, he really didn't have any idea why he'd done it. It had just been one of those things that had seemed like a good idea at the time. And then later on? It had seemed like the worst idea he'd had in his life.

"We don't have anywhere to go though," said Jamie.

"Come with us," said Matt, without really thinking it through. The words just tumbled out of his mouth.

"Come with you where?"

"We're headed to Damian's mom's house. We're going to hole up there."

"Uh, all right."

"Help me gather some stuff," said Matt, his mind not focusing on the social implications of what he'd offered, but instead on the list of things that he needed to gather up before they left for Damian's mom's house. "There's food in the kitchen. Get whatever you can. Make sure to get everything from the freezer and the top cabinets."

"All right," said Jamie and Mia together.

Without a word, Matt disappeared into the bedroom. He headed to his safe in the closet, unlocked it, and took out his Glock.

He checked it over, and loaded it. It felt good to load it, and it felt good to have the weight of the Glock in his hand.

He also had a holster in the safe, and he took a minute now to fit it into the waistband of his pants. He untucked his work shirt, letting it hang out so that it covered the Glock.

He checked his profile in the mirror, and while he looked a little funny with the long shirttails hanging down, the Glock and its holster didn't print at all on the shirt. It was invisible, which was just the way he wanted it.

Next, Matt grabbed a flashlight from his nightstand, and a couple other odds and ends from here and there.

He really didn't have that much stuff in his apartment. Back before he'd moved out here, he'd been contemplating buying a bunch of camping gear, since camping was the sort of activity he wanted to spend more time doing. In the end, he hadn't bought the gear, and instead of camping he'd spent his outdoor time in New Mexico hiking on the weekends.

But now he wished that he'd made the investment in that camping gear. After all, who knew how long this would all go on. And who knew where they'd end up.

In the back of his mind, Matt had the idea that Damian's mom's house was just a stopgap measure. Maybe they could wait it all out there. And maybe not.

Back in the kitchen, Matt found Jamie and Mia jamming food into large black trash bags. The freezer door was open, letting some chill into the room.

"Good work," he said, grabbing the last of the frozen dinners from the freezer and jamming them into a bag. Then he took the bag, tied it up, and slung it over his shoulder. "Come on. We'd better be getting out of here."

Only when the three of them were out in the hallway did Matt think that it was a little weird that he had offered to let Jamie hole up with him and Damian. After all, he hadn't spoken to her at all since that very awkward incident..

And he hadn't even asked Damian if it would be OK.

"Are you sure this is going to be OK with Damian and his mom?" said Jamie. Apparently she was thinking along the same lines.

"Yeah. Damian's a good guy... And he knows you from the office... I'm sure it'll be fine."

Matt noticed that Jamie and Mia didn't seem to have any other ideas about where to go. They didn't put up too much of a fuss about being an inconvenience or anything like that, so they must have been pretty desperate.

Which he could understand.

He didn't even hold it against them for breaking into his apartment.

Hell, he might have done the same, if he'd been in their shoes.

The three of them made their way through the hallways, carrying the trash bags.

Matt didn't spot the neighbor who'd called out to him through the door. And he didn't spot anyone else either.

In fact, they didn't see anyone. The hallways were as empty as they had been when he'd come in, and he wondered if the anonymous "neighbor" was misinformed, or perhaps lying.

It didn't really matter. The building definitely wasn't a good place to ride out a virus crisis.

"Did you two see anyone when you came in?" said Matt.

They both shook their heads.

"Not a soul," said Mia.

He noticed that he felt better, just knowing that he had his Glock on him.

Of course, now that he had the Glock, there might come a time when he'd have to make difficult decisions. For instance, if a potentially contaminated person was coming at him, did he have a right to shoot them?

Yes. The answer was definitely yes. But that didn't mean that it'd be an easy decision. Taking a life was serious, and while he thought that he had what it took do to it, he'd heard of plenty of stories of people freaking out and choking up when the time came to defend themselves.

He didn't think he'd be like that, but he also couldn't know for sure. No one could. Not until it happened.

But all in all, he'd rather face difficult decisions than be without a firearm. He'd rather be the one making the difficult decisions than letting it fall into someone else's hands.

The New Mexican sun was bright when they made it out through the big double doors into the parking lot.

"I thought you said your friend was out here?" said Jamie, a trash bag slung over her shoulder, panting a little from holding it there. She must have had one of the heavier ones, since Matt's didn't weigh as much.

"Here, give me that one," he said, holding his out, offering a trade.

"Thanks," she said, as they switched bags.

Hers had been a little heavier than his, and he slung it over his shoulder. After doing his functional training though for quite a while now, a trash bag full of frozen food wasn't really serious weight to him. He was used to cinder blocks chained together with thick heavy steel chains.

"Awww, how cute," said Mia in a funny voice. "You two will be back together in no time. Already looking out for each other."

Matt gave her a puzzled look. It seemed like a strange thing to say, especially considering how serious the circumstances were.

"Shut it, Mia," hissed Jamie. Then, to Matt, she said. "She's really pretty normal most of the time... she just..."

"I hope I'm not going to regret telling you two to come along with me... this is serious... we've got to be aware of danger..."

"Hey, where's your friend anyway?" said Mia, apparently

somewhat flighty, and already having moved on to the next thing on her docket, which was looking for Damian. "I don't see anyone here."

Matt stopped talking, instead focusing all his attention on scanning the parking lot.

It was true. It was completely empty. There wasn't a soul. It looked just as empty as it had when he and Damian had arrived.

"Damian!" he called out, taking a risk in making some noise. "Damian. Are you here?"

"Just let everyone know we're here, why don't you?" said Jamie.

"So I can see you're not going to hold back on your opinions, despite me providing you with a place to stay... with you breaking into my apartment..." Matt couldn't help it. He was annoyed.

"You know that's not my style," said Jamie, looking right at him. And he could swear that he thought he saw the hint of a smirk.

"Fair enough," he said. "Help me look for him. He's got to be here somewhere."

"We'll find him," said Mia, dropping her garbage bag on the ground, and running off through the few parked cars that were there. "Don't worry."

"What's with her? Is she nuts or something?"

"No... she's just... I don't know how to describe it. She's pretty reasonable most of the time. I mean, she's trying to help. She's just a little... different, I guess."

"Seems kind of flighty to me," said Matt.

"That might describe her."

"Hey," came Mia's voice moments later, drifting across the parking lot with some urgency.

"It looks like she's behind that parked car over there," said Jamie.

The two of them dropped their trash bags and rushed over, sprinting across the parking lot.

When they got around to the other side of the car, they saw Mia crouching over Damian, who was lying on the ground, clutching his face.

"Damian, buddy, what the hell happened?" said Matt, quickly dropping to Damian's side, kneeling down next to him.

"Some guys jumped me," said Damian.

"Jumped you? For what?"

"They thought I was someone else. I don't know. It didn't make sense. In the end, they just took my phone and my wallet."

Jamie had knelt down next to Mia, and Matt was pleased to see that she was systematically checking Damian for injuries. It showed that she had a practical side, and that she could think on her feet.

"Looks like you're going to be OK," said Jamie. "They didn't get you that bad."

"It really hurts though," moaned Damian.

"Stop being such a baby," said Mia. "Come on. Get up. We're going to your mom's house." She held out her arms, offering them to him as if to help him up.

"Who's she?" said Damian, looking confused.

Suddenly, a horrible thought occurred to Matt. What if the men who'd attacked Damian had been infected?

"These attackers..." said Matt. "Did you get a look at them? Their veins?"

"They weren't infected," said Damian, speaking somewhat curtly.

"You saw their veins then?"

"Yeah. I got a pretty good close-up when they were beating me senseless. I mean, I didn't ask them to see. Like, hey, man, mind if I check to see if your veins are dilated before I permit that you beat me on the body and the head? No, it wasn't like that it."

"But you managed to see their veins?"

"It wasn't hard. They were right up against me. I saw their necks... the backs of their hands... totally normal.... not enlarged at all..."

"Are you telling the truth?" said Mia, her voice sounding high-pitched in comparison to Damian's.

"Who's she again?" said Damian, looking annoyed. "Yeah, lady, I'm telling the truth."

"She's Mia," said Matt. "Jamie's friend. Roommate, I mean. Here, let me give you a hand."

Matt grabbed onto Damian roughly and pulled him to his feet.

His face was bloody, and it looked like his nose might have been broken, but other than that he was OK.

Matt filled him in briefly on the new plan. "I figured that'd be OK with your mom," he added.

"Yeah, I guess so," said Damian. "Come on. Let's get the hell out of here. I know a good way to get there from here. I'll lead the way."

Wiping the blood away from his face, Damian took off, walking rapidly across the parking lot, heading towards the street.

"We'll be right behind you," called out Matt. "We've got to get the bags of food."

Damian didn't stop or slow down. Apparently he was pissed off about the mugging and just wanted to get the hell out of there. As far as Matt could tell, it was understandable.

"Why don't you catch up to him?" said Matt, speaking to Mia. "Jamie and I will grab the bags of food."

"OK," said Mia brightly, immediately starting to half-skip, half-run towards Damian.

Jamie gave a little laugh as she watched her friend dash off.

"She's a little... weird, isn't she?" said Matt.

Jamie just made a noncommittal noise of agreement. "Hey," he said, as they made it back to the bags of food, grabbed them, and shouldered them. Matt had two of them and Jamie had one of them. "Can I ask you a question?"

"Sure," said Matt, expecting a question about their dating history, about why he'd given her a key, or about why they hadn't spoken at all at the office since their last date.

But instead, she asked him something completely different. "Do you trust Damian?"

"Trust Damian? What do you mean?"

"About the mugging."'

"You think he didn't get mugged. You think he just beat himself up or something?"

"No, I mean about the veins of the attackers. Maybe they were infected. I know it crossed your mind. Or else you wouldn't have asked him about the veins."

"Yeah, I thought it was a possibility," said Matt. "But I mean, I know Damian. He wouldn't lie about that. Not about a life-or-death situation like that..."

"Even if it was his own life?" said Jamie. "Even if he were lying to save his own life?"

Matt didn't know what to say. So he let the question hang in the air as they walked, trash bags over their shoulders, across the parking lot towards the street.

Would Damian really have done something like that?

Would he really lie to save his own skin?

Matt thought about what he himself might do. He already knew the answer. He wouldn't lie if it meant jeopardizing anyone else. He just knew it in his bones. That wasn't the sort of person he was.

And Damian?

Well, he was pretty sure Damian wouldn't do that.

Maybe not 100 percent sure.

But what choice did Matt really have? He had to trust his friend. There was no other option.

9

J udy was a tough woman. She didn't take shit from anyone.

Well, anyone except her son, Damian.

Her only son.

He was a good kid. Not really a kid, at all. He was in his late twenties. Twenty-nine to be exact. But he'd always be a kid to her.

For some reason, Damian had just never really seemed to get his life together. Before he'd gotten this most recent office job, she'd been really worried about him. She'd had him come back and live with her to try to help stabilize him for a while.

She thought that maybe she'd made a huge mistake. After all, she wasn't a proponent of adult kids living at home with their parents. Not unless there were special circumstances.

But she just had such a soft spot for him that she let it all slide. And now that he was doing so well with maintaining a job, she didn't want to mess it all up for him by destabilizing him.

Judy knew she was being silly. She knew she was being weak, and she knew that she was turning a blind eye to her son's irresponsible tendencies. She wouldn't have put up with some of his behavior coming from anyone else.

She had too much of a soft spot for him. She knew that. She didn't quite accept it though, and she still got upset about it, still got mad at herself about it.

Judy had never liked computers much, but she was sitting in front of one now. A desktop computer. Ancient by modern standards. But it still worked. Still connected to the internet.

It didn't display all the fancy pages with their fancy graphics. But it still worked fine for the news sites.

So Judy had read all the latest on the virus. She knew that the authorities had identified that dilated veins were a symptom of infection during the silent period.

The latest news was that the dilated veins didn't show up for twelve hours. And within that twelve-hour incubation period, the virus did not appear to be contagious. The authorities used the word "appear" because they weren't sure. Normally, it took months, if not years, to understand a virus, to understand how it worked. But H77 had showed up spontaneously, without warning. There hadn't been time to study it.

The fact that the virus had a twelve-hour window in which it wasn't contagious did not mean that huge numbers of people weren't infected.

The flight from Beijing to New York had been well over twelve hours, meaning that, given what was now known about the airborne transmission of H77, nearly everyone on the plane was infected.

With most viruses, there was usually a small percentage of the population that was naturally immune. With H77, it seemed that number might be as small as five percent. But it was, as of yet, impossible to say with certainty.

The authorities were careful to stress that there was no way to know if one was as of yet immune, so the best strategy for avoiding death was complete avoidance, complete quarantine.

What irked Judy to no end was the strategy that the City of Albuquerque seemed to be taking. The local news sites were reporting that many apartment buildings and houses were being cleared out and evacuated by the city officials. People were being taken to the downtown stadium for a "quarantine" program.

While the city officials didn't seem to see anything wrong with their plan of grouping everyone together, the people in the comments section at least saw something wrong with it. They were vicious, calling the city officials out for maybe the worst plan that anyone had ever come up with.

"Yeah," wrote one person. "Get every potentially sick person together. Take them out of their private residences.... the only advantage to this idiotic plan is that the virus will spread fast, like wildfire... we won't have to wait around long to meet our makers..."

From Judy's perspective, the commentator was right on.

There were plenty of other commentators, writing about how they weren't going to leave their houses or apartments, about how they were going to put up a fight, about how the city officials would have to pry their firearms from their cold dead fingers.

Judy's hand went automatically to the .44 Magnum lying on the table next to her. The first thing she'd done when she'd seen the news about the virus was head to the safe and take out her gun.

Judy may not have used the Magnum in a few years, but she'd still made sure to keep it in good condition. She'd done everything that the gun required, and maybe a little more.

And while she may have been out of practice, she doubted that she'd have any trouble hitting anything. She'd grown up with guns in the house, and she still had clear memories of her father teaching her sister and her how to shoot.

Judy's thoughts turned for a moment towards her sister, who had died of breast cancer just a few months ago. She and Damian had traveled together to the funeral up in Washington State, where her sister had settled a couple decades ago with her now-deceased husband.

There was a knock at the door. A loud knock.

A hundred thoughts flashed through Judy's mind. Was if it was the city officials? Had they come for her?

Or was it Damian? He should have been here by now.

Or was it someone else?

This wasn't Judy's first time around the block, and she wasn't nearly naive enough to think that the virus was going to be the only problem in the next few days.

Judy had a good understanding of human nature, and she understood that people were vicious when push came to shove. They'd do what they thought necessary to save themselves and their families.

Judy's hand went to her gun, grasping it around the barrel. The cool metal felt good in her hand.

The gun was solid. Well made. An honest product, one that you knew wasn't going to break on you when you needed it most. It didn't seem like there were many consumer products left these days that the same could be said for.

Judy took the gun with her as she stood up, her hands

sliding around it until her hand was around the handle in a good grip.

Another loud knock.

Judy wasn't the sort of person to avoid problems. If there was something to deal with, then she dealt with it. With the one true exception being Damian.

But he was a good kid. And he was doing a lot better. Sure, there were things that Judy wished Damian had done, like learn how to shoot a gun, or settle down with a good woman, but she was sure those things would come in time. If they made it through this virus outbreak, that is.

The house wasn't large, and Judy made her way through it quickly.

She stood to the side of the front door. If someone somehow opened the door from the outside, there was plenty of room for the door to swing open on its hinges.

She got the revolver into position, pointing it at what would become the door's opening.

"Who is it?" she yelled out, her finger sliding onto the trigger.

"Mom! It's me."

It was unquestionably her son's voice.

Her heart slowed down a little in her chest.

But all wasn't yet well. Not until she knew what was going on for sure.

"Who's with you?" she called out. "Are you alone?"

"No. I told you. Matt from work is here."

Judy had met Matt once or twice. He seemed like a good guy. Certainly had his life together more than her son.

"Anyone else?"

"Two girls. From work. Well, one's from work, and the other is her roommate."

Judy was listening carefully to her son's voice. He

sounded stressed, but not unduly so. It certainly didn't sound like someone was pointing a gun to his head, trying to gain access to the house.

Judy hadn't wanted to look through the peephole since she knew that a bullet of a certain caliber could easily pierce the door. Someone on the other side could call out, wait until they saw darkness appear in the peephole, and fire at the door, killing Judy instantly.

But now it seemed like it was worth the risk.

In the peephole, Judy saw her son standing there. Three figures behind him. No guns drawn. Nothing too dangerous looking.

She figured it was safe.

And then she remembered.

What if they were infected?

"Any of you infected?" she called out.

"No. Of course not. Come on, mom. Let us in. There are all these weird people out here on the streets... we've got to get inside..."

"Not until you show me your veins!"

"You're going to pull this? On your own son? You think I'd come in here and infect you?"

"Do it! Or you're not coming in."

Judy may have thought that she often went too easy on her son, Damian, but she did realize that others may have looked at it differently. In other people's eyes, she was just as harsh on him as she was on anyone else.

"You first, Damian!" she shouted through the door. "Hold the backs of your hands up. Close to the peephole."

She could hear Damian groaning and grumbling on the other side of the door. But he did it. He held up his hands.

"A little closer," she shouted through the door, her hand never leaving her pistol.

Damian's hands looked clean.

"Next!" she shouted. "You know the drill. Quick now!"

One by one, Damian's three companions showed their veins to the peephole.

When it was all over, Judy didn't waste any time. She threw the deadbolt open and swung the door open wide. She stood to the side, pistol in hand, as they trudged through the door.

"Nice to see you again, Mrs. Jones," said Matt, who always seemed to have his manners about him.

"You know you can just call me Judy," said Judy.

"Sure thing, Judy."

While Damian threw himself down on a nearby chair, panting heavily, apparently from exertion, Matt introduced the two young women. One of whom was Damian's coworker and the other was her roommate. The coworker seemed to have her wits about her, but Judy wasn't yet sure about the roommate, who seemed either a little ditzy or a little strange.

"We brought food from my place," said Matt, pointing to the trash bags that they'd dumped in the corner. "Hopefully we won't be too much of a burden while we wait this thing out... my apartment didn't seem like a good place... lots of doors and windows and shared walls..."

"From what I can tell, they're evacuating a lot of apartment buildings," said Judy.

"That's what they tried to do to us," said Jamie, before briefly explaining how she and her roommate had had to jump off a school bus to avoid being taken to what amounted to a detention center.

"I was just reading about that on the computer," said Judy. "About how they're taking everyone to the stadium and putting them together... the way I see it, what better way to make sure the virus spreads?"

"Our thoughts exactly," said Matt.

"Well, I know one thing for sure. I'm not leaving this house." She held up her revolver, her finger outside the trigger guard. "And if they try to make me, I'm going to make it very difficult for them."

Matt let out a little chuckle. "We're with you on that. Like I said, we really appreciate you letting us stay here for a little while. Hopefully all this crazy virus stuff will be over soon enough... hopefully they'll get it contained."

"I wouldn't put too much stock in that theory," said Judy. "I've been alive a little longer than you, which means I've had more years to watch as the 'authorities' and 'experts' in whatever category screw everything up time and time again.... You three are welcome to stay here as long as necessary. I could use some help around here anyways as someone," she pointed to her son Damian, who was slouching in the chair, "never seems to have the time to help his mother with anything."

"We appreciate that," said Matt. "I'll get this food into the kitchen, then."

Judy, strange as it seemed, was already glad that her son had brought over friends. She was already appreciating Matt's approach. He seemed eager to help out. Eager to do things. Matt and Jamie were already hauling the extra food down the hall to the kitchen. In contrast, Damian just had managed to slouch further down in his chair.

"Do you like gardening?" said Mia, out of the blue, her voice taking on a lilting kind of quality to it.

Judy didn't know what to make of the question. She shot her son a look, hoping he could help her interpret this strange young lady's out-of-context question.

But he just shrugged his shoulders.

"I really like to garden," Mia was saying, apparently content to not receive an answer. "My job doesn't let me do a lot of it... It's just the way it is, I suppose."

"Yes, that can be tough," said Judy. "But we've got more important things to worry about right now. Why don't you and Damian go down to the basement and see if you can find some flashlights and candles and things like that?"

"The power's not off though," groaned Damian. "And you never clean that basement. It's gross down there."

"The power might go off soon," said Judy. "If a large percentage of the population dies from the virus, then there isn't going to be anyone left to work the power plants or manage the electrical grid."

"The basement sounds like fun!" said Mia brightly, standing up. "Come on, Damian. This'll be great."

"Ugh," groaned Damian, standing up reluctantly.

"What am I going to do with him?" muttered Judy to herself as she watched the two of them disappear down the hallway towards the basement door.

As they disappeared, as if on cue, a siren sounded in the street.

Judy stopped and listened to it. At first, she thought that it might be an ambulance or police car on another street, heading away from her house.

But the siren sound only got louder.

Was it a police car or an ambulance?

There weren't any windows by the door, and the peep-hole didn't do her any good.

It sounded more like a cop car, but for some reason, she couldn't remember if the siren sounds were different.

"What's that?" said Matt, appearing near her in the hall-way. "Cop cars?"

Judy was surprised to find herself relieved to see him. Not that she couldn't handle things on her own, but Matt standing there gave the impression of a solid and reliable individual. Someone you could count on.

"I can't tell. You think it's the police or an ambulance?"

"I think it's the police," said Matt, after a pause to listen carefully to the sirens.

"That makes sense."

"It does?"

"Maybe they're coming to kick us out."

"But that doesn't make any sense. Why would they do that?"

"Why did they do it to your friends? Just because it doesn't make sense doesn't mean it's not happening."

The two of them fell into a brief silence, over which the sound of the sirens only grew louder.

Judy's house was the second from a dead-end cul-de-sac. If the police were going to evacuate the street, they'd probably start with the last house and then work their way down the street. If that were the case, Judy wouldn't have much time before they arrived at her house.

10

DAMIAN

"Wow, this is so cool..." said Mia, her voice sounding strange and distant.

"Cool?" said Damian. "What's going on with you? It's just a basement. Are you always like this, or are you just getting weirder since I met you or something?"

Damian knew that he didn't always have a lot of tact, so sometimes he just chose to go with his brash gut instincts of speaking his mind.

"I don't think it's weird to appreciate things," said Mia.

"Yeah, it's not. But this is just an old cramped basement."

"It's that... but so much more..."

"Are you high or something?" said Damian. How could someone be this strange? It didn't make sense.

"Maybe a little."

"A little?" said Damian, his voice not hiding his shock. "What the hell is wrong with you? What are you on?"

"Just a couple pills."

"What? Are you nuts? Are you an addict or something? This isn't a good time to be using drugs."

"I'm not an addict," she said, wistfully. "I just like to take the..."

"What? Don't say you like to experience a world full of wonder... see the beauty in everything... those cliches are a little too tired at this point, you know?"

"I was going to say that I just needed to take the edge off... they're just anxiety pills... it's just that I took a couple more than I'm supposed to... I bought them from this girl at work..."

"Those things aren't good for you," said Damian. "And now you're not useful. You're all hopped up on that shit. Come on, we've got to try to find the flashlights."

"Oooohh," she said, gazing in amazement at a pair of dirty old skis in the corner. "Were these your skis?"

"No," said Damian shortly. "Come on. Can't you do anything? Even if you're on those pills, you could still try to help me."

"I'm often more of an emotional help," said Mia. "A lot of people tell me that they feel safe talking to me."

"Maybe that's because it doesn't seem like you're going to remember anything."

Mia made a strange noise, sort of a cross between a cat's purr and a little yelp.

"Weirdo," muttered Damian, as he pushed his way through some old cardboard boxes that had been sitting there for at least a decade, making his way further back into the basement.

It was dark in the basement, and it felt completely shut off and separate from the rest of the house. Whereas the rest of the house was clean, there were spiderwebs everywhere down here.

The basement hadn't been cleaned since probably

before Damian had been born. More and more things had just been continuously added to it.

Occasionally, when he'd been a kid, his mom had made him come down here to the basement with the explicit instructions of either retrieving something or organizing a small corner.

More often than not, Damian had found some way to goof off rather than doing what he'd been told.

But recently, as Damian understood it, his mom had been coming down here more and more. She'd been been doing what he'd called hoarding, and what she'd called simply gathering useful things and good supplies.

There it was. Over there in the corner. A whole metal shelf from Home Depot filled with gear. Odds and ends. There was a whole shelf full of candles and matches. Another with big tubs of what looked like rice. There was quite a bit of nonperishable food. There was even, to Damian's surprise, a fifteen-gallon tub of coconut oil.

What was it that his mom had wanted him to get? Flashlights or something like that? Surely the food could stay down here in the basement.

There were some flashlights on the top shelf, and Damian grabbed a couple of them at random and stuffed them into the pockets of his work slacks.

He was about to turn around to head back upstairs, when, off in the corner, his eye caught a dusty old mirror that had been stuck there who knew when.

The mirror was so dusty that it didn't reflect anything at all, except some vague light.

The mirror made him think about his appearance.

He moved over to the mirror, which was difficult.

"Shit," he muttered, as he knocked over a lamp. It fell

sideways to the floor, its ancient light bulb shattering on the concrete floor.

"What are you doing over there?" said Mia from across the room. She was holding a mop like a staff and had one of his mom's funny old hats on her head with an ancient fanny pack around her waist.

Damian didn't bother answering her.

He managed to get to the mirror. With one hand, he wiped off a circle of dust.

He ducked down a little and positioned his head so that he could see, craning his neck to see the veins on his neck.

Nothing. They looked totally normal. Just like the backs of his hands.

He held up his hands again, closer to his face this time.

Nothing.

They looked normal.

Not dilated at all. Not enlarged.

If he'd only still had his cell phone, he would have taken a picture of his neck. Just to be sure. And to have something to compare a later picture to.

"What are you doing over there?" said Mia, her voice still sounding very strange.

Before he could answer, she'd started stomping across the basement to him. She didn't seem to notice or care that she was walking into all manner of things, knocking them over, somehow managing to stay upright herself.

"What was that?" she muttered, as she kicked an old broken vacuum cleaner aside. It made a terrific noise as it collided with some old metal cookware that was lying haphazardly on the floor.

She was panting when she got over to Damian.

He looked at her like he couldn't believe anyone would be that strange. Or act that weird.

"What are you doing over here?" she said again.

"I guess you're not going to leave me alone until I answer you."

"No," she said, simply and matter-of-factly. "I'm not going to."

She then proceeded to stared at him with her vacant eyes and small pupils.

"You know what," muttered Damian. "You're so messed up on drugs I bet you're not going to remember this anyway. And it'll feel good to tell someone."

As he said those words, he realized that it would feel really good to get this all off his chest. It had been eating him up ever since he'd gotten mugged. He hadn't told anyone. Not even Matt. And he'd always told Matt, if not everything, plenty about his life.

It would only get worse. If Damian kept it all inside and didn't tell anyone, he'd just go crazy with anxiety.

If he told Matt or his mom, however, he didn't know what would happen. What he feared most of all was that they would become angry with him. Angry for exposing the whole group to the virus. Potentially.

Damian was scared that his own mother would throw him out of the house if he admitted what had happened.

"You're not going to tell anyone, are you?"

"No," she said wistfully. "I'm not going to tell anyone anything."

"OK," said Damian. "Here it goes. You know how I was mugged?"

She nodded but her eyes didn't show any recognition. She was already pretty messed up on the drugs. Pretty out of it.

Perfect. Just what Damian wanted. To technically tell someone, but not *actually communicate* the idea to them.

"Well," he said. "I lied about it..."

"You lied?" she said, her voice child-like and reproachful.

Damian paused. He almost didn't continue. But then he decided to go for it. "Two men attacked me," he said. "And one of them... he had his hands on me... I could clearly see the veins in his hands... and they were big... and I mean *big*... definitely not just normal... he was definitely infected.... but I mean..."

"The guy who attacked you was infected with the virus?" said Mia, repeating the words back to him in a hollow way, as if she didn't understand their meaning.

Still, having the words come back at him felt like an attack.

Damian felt like he had to defend himself.

"It's not like everyone gets infected," he said. "I mean they don't even have that kind of data out yet... but if it's anything like other viruses, then it's not anywhere near 100 percent of the people that come in contact..."

Damian found himself trailing off.

Mia was silent, but she watched him with her big eyes. She didn't take her eyes off him.

"I mean, what do you think? You think I like possibly exposing my mother and my friends to a deadly virus? No, not at all. But what choice do I have? I mean, at some point, I've got to look out for number one, right? That's me, and no one else is going to do that for me. Not even my own mother. So I mean, yeah, I'm putting you all potentially at risk. But it's really not that bad. It just depends how you look at the whole thing. Trust me, the first sign of enlarged veins on my hands, I'm out the door. I'll leave you all behind. And that means that if I do have the virus, you won't all be at risk for contamination..."

Damian was interrupted by his mother's voice. She was yelling from the top of the dark basement stairs. "Damian!" she was shouting. "We need you up here. Now! Bring the hatchet!"

"The hatchet? What?" he called back.

But there was no answer.

A hatchet? What did she want a hatchet for? Why did she sound so urgent?

"We'd better get up there," said Mia. "She sounds upset."

"Sure," Damian said. "But you're not going to tell anyone about what I said, are you?"

"Of course not," she said, her voice light and lilting.

"Good," said Damian. "Because I don't think they'd understand as well as you did."

Damian made his way towards the base of the stairs, grabbing an old rusty hatchet along the way.

He knew that it was true. If his mother or the others found out that he'd possibly been contaminated, he'd be in big trouble. He didn't know exactly what they'd do, but he didn't want to find out.

He was sure that it'd all be fine. How could he really be contaminated? There was just no way.

But, despite his best efforts to convince himself that everything was OK, Damian didn't feel like everything was OK. His body felt on edge, and kind of shaky, as if he had low blood sugar. His heart seemed to be beating much faster than normal in his chest, but for some reason he was keenly aware of each and every beat.

"Come on," said Damian, holding out his hand for Mia as he took his first step up the dark, rickety basement staircase.

11

MATT

"What are we going to do?" whispered Judy.

They were standing on either side of the dining room window. The curtains were drawn, and they both had their ends of the curtain pulled a little ways back so that they could see outside to the street.

"We're not going out there, that's what we're doing," whispered Matt.

"What's going on?" said Damian loudly, appearing behind them.

"It took you long enough," hissed Judy. "Did you get the hatchet?"

"Yeah," said Damian, tossing a rusty hatchet casually onto the dining room table made of fine wood. "What the hell did you need this for anyway? It's not like we're going to be chopping wood."

Mia, who was standing behind him, started to laugh uncontrollably.

Matt and Jamie exchanged looks, both their eyebrows raised.

"There's someone out there," whispered Judy. "You need

to be quiet, Damian. This is serious. We need that hatchet. It's a weapon..."

"A weapon?" sneered Damian. "You've got a gun, don't you? And Matt has one too."

Matt and Judy had already compared notes on their firearms. Matt was, to be frank, quite impressed that Judy was a gun owner. Not to mention the fact that he was impressed with her choice of firearm.

Matt, not having spent much time with Judy and Damian together before, was somewhat shocked at how Judy interacted with her son. She came across as a no-nonsense woman, but with her son, it was clear that she had a very high tolerance for his antics and annoying habits.

If anyone else, for instance, had come in and talked to Judy like that, they likely would have had hell to pay. Anyone except her own son, that is.

"This is serious," hissed Matt. "We heard a siren. Thought it was a police siren. But then we saw the car... just a regular beat-up old sedan. They're inside the house next door..."

"So what?" said Damian, strolling over and jostling his way into the position that Matt had taken by the window. Matt stepped aside, giving Damian room to pull the curtain far back.

"Don't do that," hissed Matt, taking the curtain from Damian by reaching around his back. "We don't want them to know we're in here."

"What's the big deal? The cops have some business next door. Doesn't concern us, right?"

"Not right," said Matt.

"At first we were worried that they were going to try to take us somewhere..." said Jamie. "... evacuate us like they did to Mia and me in our apartment, but then we realized that they're not likely real cops."

"They didn't have any uniforms on," pointed out Judy, still peering out her little slice of the window.

"So what?" said Damian. He sounded annoyed, and Matt couldn't see why he'd be so annoyed at all this. "What's the big deal? There are some undercover cops next door. Someone tell me how it affects me, or else I..."

Damian was interrupted by a loud, forceful knock on the door.

"Police," came the deep male voice. "Open up!"

Everyone stared at each other with looks of shock on their faces.

How had the man outside gotten to the front door without Judy and Matt spotting him through the window?

"Why didn't we spot him?" whispered Judy.

"I don't know," whispered Matt.

"I'll get the door!" said Mia, speaking brightly and loudly. She sounded excited at the prospect of having company.

"What the hell's wrong with you?" hissed Damian. "Help me. Grab her."

Jamie grabbed her roommate and held her close to her body. "What's the matter with you? You didn't take pills again, did you?"

"She's on drugs?" said Judy.

Matt didn't know what to make of Mia, but he knew that he couldn't deal with the situation right now. Not when there was a more pressing issue at the front door.

"Everyone stay in here," he said. "I'll handle this."

Matt's mind was running through the possibilities as he made his way to the door.

When he got there, he approached the peephole as

quietly as he could. He was well aware of the possibility that this wasn't a real cop. He was also very aware that a bullet could pierce this door easily. He didn't want someone to know that he was on the other side of it.

He looked through the peephole.

A man in plain clothes stood there.

The man had a peculiar face. Long hair hung in curtains around it. He had about a five days' growth of a beard.

There were acne scars on his skin, and eyes that were sunken deep into his face.

One of his front teeth was visible and noticeably blackened.

This didn't look anything like a cop.

Not the kind of cop that Matt had seen before, anyway.

But then again, undercover cops were often chosen for the simple fact that they did not look like cops. That, and because they had the other skills needed to perform a highly difficult and dangerous job.

Matt stepped carefully and quietly away from the door. He stood against the wall, so that none of his body was in front of the door.

"Who's there?" he called out.

"Police. Open up."

"How do I know you're real a cop?" shouted Matt back.

There was a pause.

"Open up!" The voice was commanding. Authoritative.

Maybe it really was a cop.

"I'm going to need your badge number," shouted Matt. "No offense, but these are dangerous times."

There was a long pause.

"I don't have to provide that."

As soon as Matt heard those words, he knew that the man wasn't a cop.

Matt's hand went to his Glock. His fingers wrapped around the handle. He moved his shirt with his left hand and drew the gun with his right hand.

His finger rested on the trigger guard.

It felt strange to have the gun in his hand. Good, but strange.

He'd had the gun for quite a while, and he'd been to the range with it many times.

But in all honesty, he never thought he'd have to use it. Not in real life.

His life, after all, had been a good example of a normal modern life. His food had come from a store. It didn't have to be hunted. His possessions were purchased in a store. Everything was sterile. Hygienic. Pristine. There was no physical danger. Not in the normal modern world. Not in Matt's.

But that seemed to be changing.

The world was turning.

Violent, dangerous people were coming out of the wood-work, coming out from where they'd remained hidden in the shadows.

Matt didn't know who this guy was on the other side of the door, but what he did know was that he didn't have good intentions.

Matt waited, expecting to hear the man saying some-thing else. Perhaps shouting some more commands. Or maybe knocking on the door.

But instead, he heard a metallic scraping sound.

What was it?

"He's got a crowbar," shouted Judy from the other room.

"Shit," muttered Matt.

He didn't know what to do.

But he did know that a man with a crowbar could easily

get that door off its hinges and opened. It wasn't a particularly sturdy-looking door.

The scraping sound increased in volume. It sounded so close.

Matt's heart was racing. He knew he had to do something.

His grip on his Glock tightened. There was sweat on his palm, but the handle's grip was good, and the Glock didn't slide.

"Do something!" came Jamie's voice from the other room.

She was right.

Matt had to do something.

12

MARK

It had been less than a day ago when Mark's luck seemed to have run out for good.

Less than twenty-four hours ago he'd been coming out of a bender, miserably hung over, unable to sleep, wondering if he should finally put a bullet in his temple and get it all over with.

His eyes had been bloodshot. His gut had hurt, and his memory of the last two weeks had been incredibly foggy.

Froggy, his roommate and best friend, had been nowhere to be found. Maybe he'd finally packed up and headed back to Australia where he was from, just like he'd been threatening to do for the last decade or so.

When Mark and Froggy had been in their twenties, their antics had been, if not charming, at least understandable and tolerable. Their excess drinking had been written off as a product of their young age. But as the years had passed and their behavior hadn't changed, people had started to distance themselves. Former friends had become acquaintances, and the world seemed to be giving a wide berth to Mark and Froggy.

But Mark and Froggy, unable or unwilling to change their ways, had stuck together. At least they'd had each other. Through all the petty scams they'd tried to pull, through all the DUIs, the arrests for drunk and disorderly, the restraining orders from ex-girlfriends, Mark and Froggy had been there for each other. Through it all. Thick and thin. And most if it had been pretty thick.

Their lives had only gotten harder as the years had passed. With the advent of computers and cell phones, the gift card and phone card scams that they'd run together had become obsolete.

Their money had dried up, and the rent for their crummy little place on the bad side of town had increased. Their original landlord, who'd occasionally let things slide in exchange for a case of beer or some stolen watches, had died, leaving the property to his much stricter and much-less-fun son.

Things had been getting worse for years until that fateful morning of the hangover.

Without Froggy there, Mark had actually gone and gotten the one gun that he hadn't yet pawned, and decided that it was finally time. He'd written an awkward suicide note to Froggy, should he return, that was full of misspellings and sweat stains.

Mark had even tried to go through with it. He'd always fantasized about pushing the muzzle against his temple, but in the end, he'd instead gone with taking the muzzle in his mouth, wrapping his lips around the cold steel.

It had felt good in a strange, horrible way. It had felt good to finally come up with a solution to his problems and to his life.

His life had just been one giant problem. And as he

pulled the trigger, he knew that he could rest in peace. He knew that it'd all be over in a fraction of a second.

But nothing had happened.

The gun had been out of ammunition.

And he couldn't find any in the house.

None at all. Not a single round.

So he'd given up. He'd just slouched further down on the stained and disgusting couch that he and Froggy had found on the side of the road, with the stuffing coming out of the sides.

He'd sat like that for a full four hours, doing absolutely nothing, before Froggy had returned.

"So you didn't take off to Australia?" said Mark.

"Nah, not really. You know me, always taking about it, never going through with it."

"That's you all right."

"I mean, hey, I actually made it to the airport this time."

"What happened?"

"Didn't have enough money for a ticket."

Mark laughed. "You know people don't buy tickets at the airport anymore, right?"

"I thought I could fly standby or something. I heard about it on TV."

Mark laughed again. "It's all online," he said.

"We don't even have a computer though."

"They do it all on their phones these days."

"Their phones?"

Neither Mark nor Froggy had a cell phone. They'd been left behind in more ways than one by current society.

"What's with the gun?" said Froggy, pointing to the gun.

"Tried to off myself. No bullets, though."

"Huh," said Froggy, falling into silence.

Neither said anything for a couple of minutes.

Then Froggy, apparently remembering something, sprang to life, a smile lighting up his face. "You won't guess what's happened!" he said, positively beaming.

"What?" muttered Mark, thoroughly not-yet-excited.

"A virus," said Froggy. "There's some crazy virus. It was all over the TVs at the airport... there were all these announcements about it."

"A virus? What are you talking about? Like the flu or something?"

"Something like that, but much worse," said Froggy, going on to explain all he'd heard about the H77 virus.

"All right," said Mark, finally understanding the story of the virus. "But why are you so excited about this? Why are you smiling ear to ear?"

"Because this is what we've been waiting for. This is our opportunity."

"It is?"

Froggy laughed. "Back in Australia, they'd understand," he said. "I mean, look at it this way. Do you think this virus stuff is real?"

"I guess. I mean, I figure they know what they're talking about."

Froggy let out a dismissive laugh. "They're always saying there's some new super virus that's going to kill us all. What was it last year? Swine flu or something like that? Alligator flu? Who knows. Each year it's something new and it's never the end of us all."

"Ah," said Mark, not really caring one way or the other. His hand gripped the gun again, and he wished that he'd had the bullets after all.

"Don't you see?" said Froggy. "They're getting all worked up about this. They're quarantining people. They're taking them out of their homes and they're putting them all together. They're all going to have a big slumber party in the city hall and in the stadium... and all the houses...

"...will be abandoned," said Mark, finishing Froggy's sentence for him. Mark had finally understood Froggy's point.

"It's the perfect opportunity," said Froggy.

"We'll rob them blind," said Mark, his mood doing a complete one-eighty and a huge smile growing on his ugly pockmarked face. "They'll all be in the stadium or whatever, scared of some nonexistent virus... and we'll go house to house and load up on whatever we want..."

"Now you're catching on," said Froggy, slapping Mark on the side of the head playfully. "And they cops will all be busy... the city's going to be breaking out into chaos as everyone tries to evacuate... there's going to be rampant crime... it's the perfect cover for us..."

Mark suddenly felt incredibly happy. It seemed as if his life once again had purpose. There was a good feeling in his chest, where in the past, for years, there had been only a deep pit of black despair. Now his smile grew and grew until it became a joyous laugh.

Mark laughed and laughed, and Froggy joined in.

In their excitement and happiness, they began preparing. And less than a few hours later, they were in Froggy's old beat-up car, driving up and down the nicer areas of Albuquerque, looking for abandoned houses.

It was true that many houses and apartment buildings were completely abandoned.

It was also true that traffic was extremely bad.

It took Mark and Froggy seemingly forever to move small distances across the city.

The traffic made things frustrating. As did the surprisingly sparse hauls.

They'd hit five houses at this point that had been completely empty. And they'd basically come up empty-handed. There really had been nothing of value anywhere. No expensive jewelry. No firearms. No drugs or expensive booze.

Their moods had been getting progressively worse as they drove around, looking for another house to hit.

That's when Froggy had laughingly pulled over to the side of the road, opened the trunk, and pulled out a police siren that he attached to the roof of the car.

"Nice trick," said Mark. "Where'd you get it?"

"Don't worry about that. Come on, one more house. Let's hit just one more."

"Let's just go home and get drunk," said Mark. "I'm tired of this."

Mark's spirits were already once again low.

"No, come on. One more."

Froggy steered the car down a street that almost no cars on it. He was muttering to himself all the while. "Let's go to the last house here. Yeah, that looks like a good one. No, wait. That yellow one there. I remember that from some-where? Oh! That's it!"

"What's what?"

"I remember now. I once helped deliver a couch to that yellow house. It was a temp job thing for a furniture store, you know? Anyway, that yellow house was just full of all kinds of crazy expensive stuff."

"What kind of stuff?"

"All sorts of electronics. Small stuff. Costs a ton. I know where we can sell it, too, once this all blows over."

"You sure that's the house?" said Mark, somewhat skepti-cal, as he knew that Froggy's memory could be a bit hit or miss.

"Of course," said Froggy. "Now let's switch this siren on."

"What's the point of the siren anyway?"

"If anyone's at home, they'll just think we're cops."

"But... that doesn't make sense. We're going to walk into their house in these clothes and steal their electronics?"

Froggy laughed. "Man," he said. "That doesn't make sense. No. We're going to bust our way in there. If there's anyone home and they give us a problem, we'll just bust in and show them our guns."

"What if that doesn't work?"

"We'll shoot them."

"We don't have any ammo."

"That's where you're wrong."

Mark turned towards Froggy, who gave him a wicked smile. "Don't tell me you hid the ammo from me... you didn't, did you?"

Froggy gave a little cackle. "You were always talking like you were going to off yourself. Down in Oz, we consider that a serious thing when a buddy's talking like that... so I did what any good mate would do, which is take the ammo away from you."

Mark's smile started to return. "You know, Froggy," he said, clapping his friend on the shoulder. "You're not so bad. You're really not."

"Now come on," said Froggy, pulling a couple of clips out of a cargo pocket on his pants. "Let's go steal some expensive shit."

Froggy passed a clip to Mark, who took it eagerly. The clip made a satisfying sound as Mark loaded it in.

Finally, things were starting to go his way.

Finally he was going to make something of himself.

Finally he was going to be someone.

13

MIA

Mia was starting to feel pretty weird. And that was kind of strange, because normally she could handle her pills pretty well.

It wasn't like she did them all the time. Just once in a while. Just to relieve some stress.

At this point, she couldn't remember exactly what she'd taken.

Had it been the anxiety drugs? The prescription kind that she'd bought off that coworker whose name she couldn't remember? The one with the curly red hair?

Or had they been the party drugs?

Surely, she'd be able to tell the difference. After all, ecstasy always made her feel all warm and fuzzy.

Did she feel like that now? She wasn't totally sure. Everything was getting kind of muddled up and cloudy. Her thinking wasn't the same as it had been before.

In her youth, which wasn't that long ago, Mia had been somewhat of a party girl. She'd experimented with going to musical festivals, popping some pills, smoking some stuff, and generally just kicking back and enjoying herself.

Those days were gone, but not *long* gone, and she still liked to remember them sometimes, both fondly and viscerally. Chemical aid here and there didn't hurt.

Mia *was* feeling relaxed, but that could have been almost any drug.

The drugs were really kicking in. Whatever they were.

"What's going on?" she said sleepily. "Why is someone knocking on the door?"

"Shhh," hissed Damian.

"But I want to see what's going on. Why aren't you letting them in?"

Mia was somewhat aware that now that she wasn't remembering things properly.

She couldn't remember where she was or how she'd gotten there.

Was she at another house party?

Had she been to work today?

People around here had been talking. She remembered that. Something about a virus.

Was that a new type of drug? Something that had just hit the streets?

"I'm going to let them in," said Mia, speaking defiantly.

She started to move forward towards the door, which was just about the only thing visible in her haze.

"No!"

Someone grabbed her. Two strong hands on each of her arms.

Mia struggled, trying to break free.

Just then, Mia noticed someone standing next to the door. Something in his hands. A gun.

"He's got a gun!" she shrieked, suddenly breaking free and rushing towards the man.

She collided with him.

He tried to stay up on his feet. But she'd hit him with too much force, and the two of them fell down, colliding with the door as they did so.

Mia barely felt the pain in her head as it smashed into the hard door.

She tasted blood, but she was becoming dissociated, and it seemed as if the blood might be someone else's. Not her own.

And if it was her own? So what? Why was her blood so important? Did it need to stay in her body all the time? Couldn't it go out and have a little fun?

"Can't it just have a little fun?" she said, cackling.

She was really high now. Soaring through the stratosphere. Colors and shapes all around her. She'd completely forgotten that she'd taken pills. She'd completely forgotten what pills even were. Many concepts had ceased to exist for her.

"Someone help me," someone was saying, grunting.

Hands were on her, but she barely knew what hands were any more.

There was a tremendous sound nearby.

She looked up and saw the door.

It was as if it was the first time she'd ever seen a door.

And what a door to see.

It was bursting open.

Bursting open as if it was the only door that had ever existed and the only door that ever would exist.

Color swarmed through the opening as the door's hinges burst apart.

Something was coming through, something other than the colors. Something powerful.

People were screaming.

A tremendous sound went off.

Something so incredibly loud that it sounded like the heavens themselves. It sounded like thunder itself, near where it was forged high on the mountains amid the lighting.

It was a gunshot.

Someone had shot a gun.

The knowledge suddenly sobered her up, the same way a cattle prod would sober up a drunk.

Her limbs stiffened as she bolted upright.

"Someone help!" she cried out.

There were figures all around her. Some kind of intense scuffle. But she couldn't tell what had happened. She couldn't figure it out.

For Mia, the colors had all disappeared. The glory and pleasure of the experience had faded away to a dark gray kind of fuzz that seemed to permeate everything. The drug experience had once again become mere confusion rather than pleasure.

"You shot him," she cried out, not knowing who she was speaking to or who she was speaking about.

Suddenly, an idea occurred to her.

Maybe she was the one who had been shot.

After all, she knew that she was not the one who had shot the gun. She'd never shot a gun before in her life, and there was no reason to believe that she would have started today of all days.

There was something important that had happened today, but she couldn't remember it. And it was something more important than the occurrence of a fantastic or deranged house party.

Mia was searching for something. But she couldn't remember what.

Her memory was fading out again.

What had just happened?

She found her hands. Those were the things that she'd been searching for.

She held up her hands. Right in front of her eyes. Got a real clear look at them.

There was blood all over them. Bright red blood. Her hands were completely drenched in it, as if she'd dipped them in a bucket full of the stuff.

What was happening?

What had happened?

Mia didn't know.

She opened her mouth.

Wide.

A scream issued forth.

It seemed to fill the room.

The scream was a dark black cloud. It was smoke that seemed to devour the empty air around her. It filled everything. It overtook everything.

"Get her off of me, someone," said Matt.

He was trying to speak as calmly and clearly as he could. But inside he was completely losing it.

His heart was galloping away.

His blood felt hot and cold at the same time.

He was drenched in sweat.

His hair was completely soaked. His hair was plastered to his head, despite his short haircut.

Matt had just shot someone. It had happened.

He still had the gun in his hand. His palms were sweaty.

His finger was still on the trigger that he had pulled. The very same trigger that had ended the man's life.

"Someone!" said Matt, speaking a little louder and a little more urgently than before.

Mia was on her knees, her arms around Matt's legs at his knees. She was clutching him as if he were a large stuffed bear that she needed for comfort.

Her mouth was open and she was emitting a wild animal sort of moan.

Matt didn't know what was going on with her but she seemed completely delirious.

Matt's head still hurt from when she had tackled him.

It had all happened so fast. And Mia hadn't made things any easier.

It seemed that she had lost her mind. And at just the wrong moment.

Matt had been next to the door, waiting, gun drawn, when Mia had attacked him. They'd fallen into the door.

And the guy on the other side of the door had taken his crowbar to the door. It had come open, the man had stepped in.

Matt hadn't had a choice.

He'd told the man to back down. He'd told him to leave.

But instead of backing down, the intruder had drawn a gun.

That's when Matt had pulled the trigger.

Matt's body felt shaky from all the adrenaline. It reminded him of getting low blood sugar once when he'd been hiking all day without any food to speak of.

"I didn't have a choice," Matt found himself saying. "I couldn't have done it any differently..."

"You did the right thing," said someone behind him.

The door was still open. Busted open.

Matt stood just behind the opened doorway.

Jamie had rushed forward to try to get Mia off of Matt. Her hands were around Mia. "Come on, Mia," she was saying. "We've got to move.

Mia just wailed louder, apparently completely disoriented, apparently completely unaware of her surroundings.

The dead man was lying on the concrete stoop.

Matt stared at him. Stunned.

He'd never, in his wildest imagination, thought that he'd actually have to shoot someone.

Sure, he'd gone to the range. He'd bought a gun. He'd mentally prepared himself for the possibility. He'd told himself that he might have to do it some day, that he might have to kill someone.

He'd thought that he'd been prepared for killing. And, in a way, he had been. He'd been able to pull the trigger. He hadn't frozen the way some people did.

But the aftereffects were what he hadn't prepared for.

But he could dig himself out of this.

He needed to dig himself out of this.

Still, he remained frozen. Just standing there.

The dead man coughed. A horrible, weak, sick cough.

Apparently he wasn't dead.

Blood came out of the dead man's mouth and splattered on the concrete that he lay on.

Matt acted. He stepped forward swiftly, Mia falling to the wayside, and he stooped down and took the man's gun from him.

Matt's bullet had hit the man in the throat and neck area. The man's neck had exploded. Blood was everywhere. The inside of his throat was exposed and visible.

Matt couldn't believe he was alive. It didn't make sense.

The man's chest was rising and falling ever so slightly.

It looked like the world's worst surgeon had cut open the man's throat with a dull scalpel, tossing the pieces aside casually, letting them fall on the concrete stoop.

The others apparently hadn't noticed that the intruder was still alive.

"She's on drugs," Damian was saying. "She told me she was on a bunch of pills or something."

"Pills? Not again, Mia. Come on, we'd better make her throw up. I thought she was over all this."

"She's on pills? That poor thing. Is she an addict?"

"Who cares if she's an addict? She did this to herself."

"She's not an addict."

The dying man coughed again. With each labored breath, blood from his throat was splattering out into the air.

"I've got to kill him," said Matt, speaking to no one in particular. Maybe he was speaking to himself.

"He's not dead?"

"You shot him. Matt, come on back inside."

Matt didn't want to waste another round. Who knew how many more he'd need.

"Oh, shit, he's still alive!" It was Damian's voice.

Mia was still wailing.

"I can't look at it. That's disgusting!"

Someone else made a retching noise, as if they were throwing up. It might have been Jamie.

Matt knelt down, his shoes not far from the dying man's head. Reaching into his back pocket, he took out his folding knife.

With his gun still in one hand, he flicked open the knife with his thumb.

Matt had never been squeamish about blood the way some were. When he'd visited his friend's farm once, he'd killed a couple chickens and even a goat. Just a way to help out, since it'd been slaughter day. The way Matt saw it, that was just part of life.

But even so, he winced a little internally as he ran the blade's edge across the man's already slit-open throat.

More blood.

A small, strange noise.

The man's slight breathing stopped.

Behind him, Mia wailed.

"Help me get her into the kitchen."

Suddenly, Damian appeared next to Matt. "Shit," he muttered. "He's dead."

"Yes," said Matt simply. "He's dead."

"He's really dead," said Damian, his voice sounding kind of faint and strange.

Matt didn't say anything

Suddenly, Damian turned, leaned over, and vomited.

The vomiting made Matt think of the virus. "I almost forgot about the virus," he said. "I'd better check..."

Matt wiped his knife off on the dead man's dirty jeans. He got most of the blood off, but some of it remained in the joint. Matt pocketed the knife before crouching down again.

Matt figured that if the man was infected, he himself would have already been exposed.

If the virus was transmitted by air, which seemed likely, than surely it would also be transmitted by blood.

And there was plenty of blood.

So Matt threw caution to the wind and picked up one of the dead man's arms. It was loose and somewhat floppy. Rigor mortis hadn't yet set in, of course, and yet the dead man was also exerting no control over his muscles.

Had brain activity ceased? It was a random thought that popped into Matt's head as he examined the backs of the dead man's hands. He remembered reading somewhere that brain activity continued for up to ten minutes after death.

Sure, he'd read it. But that didn't mean it was true.

Maybe he'd misremembered it anyway.

Not that it mattered anyway.

"They look OK," said Matt, leaning in for a closer look. "Take a look, will you?"

"Let me see," said Damian, wiping his mouth and getting down there and taking the hand himself. "No... looks OK. Doesn't look enlarged."'

"We can't really look at the neck," said Matt, eyeing the destroyed neck.

"No, we can't. Hey. Who's that?"

Damian pointed to the street.

A car had just pulled up.

It was that same old beat-up car that had driven by earlier. In the commotion of the door being banged in, Matt hadn't noticed that the car had disappeared at all.

The car was an early '90s American-made car. Matt didn't know the make or model. The manufacturer's emblem seemed to be missing from the front of the car, near the grille.

The old beat-up car had rust on the running boards, which was extremely rare to see in New Mexico. Even though there was snow in the winter months, and the streets were salted, the air was so dry that most cars didn't rust. Some people actually came from out of state just to buy rust-free cars.

"What's that car doing?"

"It's a man... he's looking at the dead guy..."

"He's got a gun!"

Matt saw it just as Jamie spoke the words. The man's window was already rolled down, and Matt could clearly see the driver. He looked thoroughly disreputable.

More threatening than his looks though was the gun in his hand. His arm was extending, bending at the elbow, in what seemed like slow motion.

There was no doubt about it. The dead man and the man in the car knew each other.

This wasn't random. Now this was revenge.

There was anger etched into the driver's face. Clear and easy to read, even from a distance.

"Inside!" ordered Matt, his voice firm and commanding.

There was jostling. Someone stepped on someone else's foot.

"Inside!"

Matt was right behind them. He had his Glock in his hand, which was outstretched.

He knew that he wasn't going to make it inside without firing a shot.

He knew he wasn't likely to hit the driver. But he was still going to try. And even a miss would provide some cover.

Matt's finger pulled the trigger.

The gun kicked. He steadied against it.

Not a bad shot.

The bullet went into the car. Through the open window.

But no screams. No blood.

Likely not a hit.

Matt was inside the house before the driver got off a shot.

Matt didn't know where the bullet struck.

He went to slam the door closed, only to realize and remember that it was off its hinges.

"Help me with this," he said. "We've got to get this more secure."

The others put their hands on the door along with him.

They pushed it back in the door frame, finally obscuring the dead man from view.

But there was no getting the door back on its hinges. There was no locking it. No getting it closed all the way.

A car door slammed outside.

"Someone get to the window," said Matt. "We need to see where he's headed."

"I'm on it," said Judy, speaking curtly and pointedly. Her footsteps were loud on the floor.

They needed to somehow seal off this entrance, or else he doubted they'd be successful in defending Judy's house.

J amie could barely believe what was happening.

Shots had been fired.

Matt had shot someone. Killed him.

Someone else was trying to get into the house.

"Maybe we can like wedge it in there," said Damian, who, along with Matt, was pressing his body against the door.

"Wedge it in? It's never going to stay, you idiot!" said Jamie.

"Hey, don't call me an idiot."

"We need a table... the dining room table... Judy, what's he doing? You got your eyes on him?"

"He's standing in the front yard," yelled Judy, from the other room. "He looks confused, like he's trying to figure out what to do.. He's got a face tattoo..."

"Nice," said Damian. "I always wanted to get one of those. But I just didn't think I'd get hired anywhere."

"You *are* an idiot then," said Jamie.

She knew it wasn't the right time to insult his intelligence, not when their lives were on the line, but she just couldn't help herself. There was something absolutely infuriating about Damian's attitude. He was clearly a mama's boy if there ever was one, easily able to let his mother take care of all his needs. The weird thing was that his mother, Judy, just didn't seem like the type to put up with his attitude.

"We'll get the table now," said Matt. "If he's coming to the door, then we've got to move fast... Damian, you want to get the table or stay by the door?"

"Uhh..."

"Staying by the door is riskier," said Matt.

"I'll get the table then..."

"All right," said Matt, nodding towards the other room.

Damian took a couple steps, stopped in his tracks, and muttered something.

"Jamie?" said Matt. "Help him, would you?"

Mia, who was sitting cross-legged on the floor, completely useless, her eyes looking funny, suddenly let out a scream.

"Mia! What is it?"

Not speaking, Mia bolted up to the standing position.

Then, like a sprinter, she dashed forward towards the door.

It was only a few feet away from her, and in just a few moments she had collided with it.

Collided hard.

She nearly fell over, knocked backwards from the impact of her own collision.

Matt let out a grunt as he held the door in its place.

"Mia! What the hell?" shouted Jamie.

She was completely stunned. Sure, Mia went off the deep end sometimes, but normally she didn't act *this* crazy. Well, maybe there had been a few times when she had...

Mia just stood there, looking stunned, a vacant look on her face. She swayed back and forth, as if there was a very strong breeze.

"Take care of her," said Matt, giving Jamie a pointed look.

"What can I do?"

"Put here somewhere. A spare room. Somewhere where she can't hurt herself. Somewhere where you can lock her in there. We've got too much to deal with."

"He's coming towards the front door," shouted Judy, from the other room.

"Shit," muttered Matt.

As if on cue, Mia started wailing. A high-pitched horrible scratching sound. Just standing there with her mouth open towards the ceiling.

"You're going to get us all killed," said Jamie, as she grabbed Mia's arm forcefully. "Come on!"

If Jamie exerted enough force, Mia would sort of walk with her with these short shuffling steps.

There was a bedroom downstairs on the first floor. There was a good working door, but there wasn't a lock. And even if there had been one, how would Jamie have locked it from the outside? There wasn't time to take the door handle off and flip it around.

"Come on, Mia," said Jamie, clutching her friend's arm harder, pulling her along with her.

Jamie was thinking fast, trying to find somewhere to stash her friend. Her eyes cast around rapidly, looking for something. Anything.

But there were no more bedrooms.

Upstairs? What about upstairs?

It probably wouldn't work. She'd have the same problem with the door handle, which would lock from the inside.

Then, standing in the hallway, firmly grasping Mia's arm, she saw the basement door.

The lock on the basement door was the other way around, so that it locked from the outside.

Maybe it had been installed incorrectly, or maybe it was supposed to be like that. It didn't matter to Jamie.

"Come on, Mia, you're headed down to the basement."

"The basements are full of animals!" screamed Mia.

"Just shut up, would you? You're going to get us all killed."

Not far away, there was the sound of heavy furniture being dragged across the floor.

Judy was saying something frantically, but Jamie wasn't paying attention to what it was.

"Come on, Mia. There's some fun stuff down here in the basement. You'll have a good time once you're down there. Come on. I'll go first."

Jamie opened the door and took the first step downstairs.

Mia's eyes lit up at the prospect of "fun stuff," and she followed Jamie eagerly downstairs.

Jamie didn't want Mia to hurt herself on the stairs, even though her patience was wearing very thin, so she walked her all the way down to the basement's concrete floor.

"It's nice down here, isn't it?" said Jamie, trying to coax Mia down the last step. "Now you're just going to stay down here. Sit in the corner and don't do anything. Don't touch anything, OK?"

There was plenty of stuff down here for Mia to get in trouble with, but there wasn't any time to find somewhere else. There wasn't anywhere else to put her.

Plus, she didn't think Mia would hurt herself. She'd never done anything like that in the past.

"You're going to stay here, right?" said Jamie, feeling anxious to get back upstairs.

Who knew what was happening up there. She couldn't hear much. Just some loud noises like big heavy things were being dragged around. Some shouts, the words unintelligible.

"He's got the virus," said Mia, looking up at Jamie with wide eyes.

Mia was definitely still under the influence, but as she spoke these words, she seemed the most sober she had in a long while.

"The virus? Who? What are you talking about? Someone's infected?"

Mia nodded vigorously. "He told me. We were down here..."

"Who? You were down here with Damian, right?"

Mia nodded again. "The guys... attacked... had the big-time veins..." It seemed that whatever small sober part of Mia that was left was trying to communicate with Jamie.

"The guys who attacked him had enlarged veins?"

Mia, seemingly only partially capable of forming sentences, nodded her head vigorously.

"This is serious, Mia, are you sure?"

Mia nodded more.

"This isn't the drugs talking?"

Mia shook her head.

"Shit..."

She wasn't sure whether to believe Mia or not, but it did seem somewhat plausible. It was a weird thing for Mia to have come up with on her own. It was an even weirder sounding drug delusion.

Upstairs, there was a gunshot.

"Shit!"

Without another word to Mia, Jamie bolted up the stairs.

She got to the top, slammed the door behind her, and locked it, hoping that Mia would be OK down there.

Silence rang out.

No one screamed.

No one spoke.

"Everyone OK?"

No one answered.

She crept through the hallway, not knowing what to expect when she reached the small area behind the front door.

She poked her head around the corner.

Matt was standing there, gun in hand. Damian was behind him, against the wall, looking scared.

They'd dragged the large dining room table and put it up against the door, so that its end rested on the floor.

"What happened?" she hissed. She didn't want to speak too loudly, since they all seemed to be trying not to make noise.

"That guy was creeping up towards the front door," said Damian, speaking in a low volume. "Matt shot at him."

"I missed," said Matt. "What's he doing now, Judy?"

"Still back in his car," came Judy's voice from the other room.

"We've got to get more furniture to put in front of this door," said Matt. "Did you get Mia somewhere safe? I can't have her interfering. We don't know what this guy is doing. He seemed to want revenge for his buddy..."

"Did he shoot at you?"

"Yeah."

"I only heard one shot."

Matt shrugged.

"Matt," said Jamie. "I need to talk to you." She glanced over at Damian.

She really didn't know how to handle the situation. She knew that what Mia had said had at least enough truth to it to warrant some type of investigation. After all, if Damian had been infected, there was no point in worrying about getting shot, because it meant they were all dead.

Or maybe it was already too late. Who knew how fast the virus spread...

They'd said that it was only contagious when the veins were enlarged, right? But they didn't know everything. The authorities were always correcting themselves later.

"Talk to me now," said Matt. He was busy examining the door, apparently trying to figure how he could further fortify it.

"I can't. I need to talk to you in private."

She didn't know how Damian would react to this serious accusation. But Matt was his friend. He'd know how to handle it.

"Can't it wait?"

"No," she said, trying to put as much emphasis on the word as she possibly could. Finally, he looked over at her, and she tried to tell him with her eyes that this was serious.

There was some recognition there in his eyes.

"OK," he said, nodding, glancing over at Damian. "Hold down the fort, OK?" He handed his gun to his friend, who took it as if he had been handed a dead rat.

"Come on," said Matt, leading the way away from the door.

T he image of Mark's dead face wouldn't leave Froggy's mind. It was stuck there. He didn't know if it'd ever leave.

Mark had been shot in the neck. Blood everywhere. Part of Mark's body turned inside out. It was horrible. A horrible sight.

They'd been best friends. Best friends for a long time.

Sure, they'd seen some horrible things in their day. They'd committed some crimes. Some violent ones too. They'd bashed some heads in, so to speak. But you couldn't get anywhere without cracking a few eggs. That's just the way it was these days. No way around it.

So they'd seen some violence. Some nasty sights. But it had been different.

This wasn't some stranger. Some easy target. This was Mark. Froggy's best bud here stateside.

And it had been so long since Froggy had been back to Australia that the faces and names of his old friends and "colleagues" had gone blurry. Too many tall-boy beers had come between those times and now. Too many knocks on the head. Too many years and too many rough times.

Was it Froggy's fault for bringing the ammo? Was it his fault for hatching the plan?

What would Mark have said?

He would have said to hell with it all. He wouldn't have blamed Froggy. Hell, he'd probably wished that he'd come up with the plan himself.

"So what am I going to do then?" muttered Froggy to himself. One of his arms was draped over the steering wheel of the old beat-up sedan.

He'd approached the house, intending to get back Mark's body, or at least exact a little revenge.

Then they'd shot at him.

He'd said to himself that he needed to screw the whole thing and just bug off.

So he'd hightailed it back to his car and driven down the block.

But he hadn't seemed capable of getting past that stop sign there. Maybe it was his conscience, long dormant, that was coming to the surface.

He knew that Mark wouldn't have been OK with lying there out in the open like that, all shot up, all busted open so that anyone could see his guts.

Froggy took a deep breath.

This wasn't right, having Mark laid out like that.

"Shit," he muttered, adding a string of even worse curses.

There was one out. No one on this side street. Everyone was probably still freaking out about the virus.

If they hadn't been, the police would have already been called.

But the police were busy with this bogus virus scare. That meant that Froggy had some time. How long would it take before it all died down, before people forgot about the "virus" and it was business again as usual?

Probably a couple days.

A couple days...

A couple days meant freedom. It meant that Froggy could do what he wanted for a while before he had to go back into stealth mode, hiding out all day in his apartment...

He'd use that freedom for fun. And for good.

First things first, he'd retrieve Mark's body and exact his revenge on the bastards who'd shot him for no good reason...

So Mark had been breaking into their home. So what? That kind of thing happened all the time.

If they'd been so concerned about it, they should have called the cops...

Froggy laughed uproariously at the thought of them on the phone, getting a busy signal, or an overworked secretary on the other end, telling them that they were understaffed and up to their shoulders in shit from the virus...

Froggy would get his revenge. Then he'd have his fun. And then by the time all this virus nonsense was over, he'd be back at home and no one would be the wiser.

There was no reason to think that Froggy would get into any trouble after it was all over... After all, everyone in that house today would wind up dead.

Froggy was sure of that. They'd be as dead as doorknobs. Bullets to the head. Knives to the throat.

And if there was any fun to be had, he'd be sure to have it. He wasn't above torture, for instance. In the right circumstances, in the right setting, it could be wonderfully fun. For Froggy, of course. Not for the other party. But that was what it was all about. Real power dynamics at play in the physical world. Violence was the interface.

"You're getting ahead of yourself there, Froggy," he muttered to himself, as he caught himself thinking those weird, crazy far-out thoughts again. "Just stick to the basics. Wait until night falls, snort some blow, and then hit the house... they won't even see what's coming..."

Froggy knew that he needed to chill out a little. Relax until night fell, which wasn't long.

He reached back into the seat behind him, grabbed a couple cans of beer that were floating around there, and dumped them into the passenger seat.

He cracked one open, and chugged it straight down.

He felt a little better.

He grabbed another beer. Same thing. Cracked it open and straight down the hatch.

He felt a lot better.

"I'll miss you, buddy," he muttered, glancing over at the empty passenger seat. "Huh, that's weird."

For some reason, he'd found himself looking at the back of his hand that held the empty beer can.

Something about his veins looked strange. Weird.

Were they bigger than normal?

Nah.

That was just crazy.

Maybe he'd chugged the beer too fast or something. It had all gone straight to his blood.

Hell if he knew how it all worked. Nothing to worry about anyway.

Froggy, knowing that the cocaine and speed would later get him in the right mood for revenge, cracked open a third beer.

Now it was time to relax

Soon it was time for revenge.

When night came. Not too long.

17

"What is it?" said Matt, pulling Jamie into the small room that contained the washer and dryer. He closed the door. "Whatever it is, make it fast. There's a guy out there who wants to kill us."

"First of all. Did you call the cops?"

"The cops? Yeah, Judy did. Or tried to. She couldn't get through. Phone lines are all busy, both 911 and the direct line."

"Shit."

"Yeah. Now what is it?"

"It's Damian," she said, speaking quickly, as if she were out of breath.

"Damian? What about him?"

"He might be infected."

"Tell me as much as you know."

"It was Mia. She told me. I guess he told her when they were in the basement or something..."

"Mia? She's out of her mind on drugs."

"I know. I know. And I'm not sure whether I can believe her or not, but there might be something to this. When she told me this, she seemed more sober. More coherent. I think it's worth investigating. I mean, if it's true..."

"...we're all screwed," said Matt, finishing her sentence for him.

She nodded, and there was a brief silence.

It was a little strange to be alone together.

But there were things to do. Things to take care of. Threats to worry about. No time for worrying about social niceties or oddities.

"I'll take care of it," he said, finally breaking the silence. "I need you to help Judy with the door. Guarding it. We don't know what the hell that guy's doing. But it's reasonable to think he might attack... And the door isn't that sturdy. You know how to work a gun?"

She nodded.

"Here," he said, handing her the dead guy's gun. "You know it?"

"I think so," she said, examining the gun. She did it in a way that made it look like she knew what she was doing. Maybe more than she actually knew. "It's a cheapie. But it'll do. Reasonably well made, I guess."

"That's what I thought," said Matt. "Come on."

He opened the door and led the way back to the front door.

Damian was standing there, looking nervous as hell. He was still holding the Glock in a strange way.

Without speaking, Matt held out his hand, obviously asking for his Glock back. "Any sign of him?"

Damian shook his head vigorously, handing the Glock somewhat eagerly back to Matt.

Matt checked it over. It looked fine. Hadn't been fired. Always good to check. Still had ammo.

"Can I talk to you in the other room?"

"Talk to me? Huh?"

"Just do it," said Matt.

"Uh, OK."

"Jamie's going to watch the door. No sign of the man, right?"

"Right."

Damian seemed even more nervous as he led the way. Matt followed close by. He didn't take his hand off his gun.

He took him to the same room that he'd taken Jamie.

"So," said Matt. "It's come to my attention..."

"I only took a five!" said Damian.

"What?"

"I did take some money from your wallet. But it was only five dollars. I swear. I'd never take a twenty."

Damian looked like he might start sweating bullets at any minute. His face was getting all red.

"I don't know what you're talking about."

"Last week when you handed me your wallet... I was heading to the vending machine."

Matt shook his head. "That doesn't matter," he said. "I could care less about that right now. What I need to ask you is about today. About the time you were assaulted by those two men."

"Oh," said Damian, his eyes shifting back and forth. "What about it?"

Matt and Damian were standing very close to each other. Matt could smell Damian's breath, which didn't smell good. He could smell old sweat and he could even smell Damian's deodorant. It was probably closer that he'd ever been to his friend.

This was a tough conversation. It was always tough to confront people. But Matt knew that he had to do it. There was no other way. Lives were at stake.

He hadn't always been good at confronting people back in his office life. But now things were different. He knew that he needed to change the way he acted if he wanted to stay alive.

"I heard that the guys who attacked you might have been infected. Is that true?"

"Huh? True?"

Matt watched carefully. Damian's eyes no longer met his occasionally. Instead, they swerved down to the floor where they stayed fixed. He mumbled something else, something unintelligible.

"According to Mia, they were infected. Now I know you know what that means. And I also understand why you'd want to hide the fact. But here's the thing, just because you might be infected, it's not like we're going to kill you or something... But think about the group. If it's true, then you might be putting everyone at risk, including your own mother."

"It's not true though!" said Damian, still not meeting Matt's eyes. "I mean, what, Mia told you that? She's crazy? She's on some kind of insane drugs or something. You're going to believe her over me."

"I have good reason to believe her," said Matt. "Now I want you to think very carefully before you answer me. Think about your mother. If you're infected, not telling us is a death sentence for her... Do you really want to do that?"

There was a long, long pause.

"OK!" said Damian frantically. "It's true. It's true. They had big veins. But so what? That doesn't mean they're infected, does it?"

Damian was moving around nervously. Somehow, it seemed that his body odor was getting stronger and worse smelling by the second. Maybe it was his stress hormones, which were rising.

Matt felt anger rumbling up inside his guts.

He tried to contain it.

But he couldn't.

It was no use.

He tried counting to ten.

One...

Two...

Three...

But it was no use.

Without thinking, he slammed his free hand into Damian's chest.

Hard.

Damian got a weird look on his face. Stunned. His body slammed back into the drywall, which cracked above his head.

"Hey!"

Matt was already on him, pressing his body against Damian's. His free hand went towards Damian's neck, where it stayed. Not quite touching. But threatening.

"I thought you were my friend," growled Matt.

Matt hadn't felt like this in a long time. He couldn't remember the last time. He felt like an animal almost. Primal, in a way. Strong. Like a man.

It would have all sounded cheesy to him last week. Or even yesterday at the office.

But now?

Now this stuff mattered. This wasn't all a big joke. Or a game. This was real life. Life or death.

"I am your friend! I was just scared. Matt, please don't tell my mom. She's going to kill me."

"Not if I do it first!" growled Matt, his hand pressing now

against Damian's neck. Pressing pretty hard. "Now we don't know how this all works. But if you're infected and you're contagious..."

"But I wouldn't be contagious yet!" squealed Damian.

"You're pathetic," growled Matt. "You make me sick. Now if you're contagious, then you've already killed us all... I need to figure out what to do."

Matt knew it wouldn't do any good to hurt Damian. In fact, if it turned out that Damian was going to live despite the threat of the virus, then hurting him would just hurt Matt and the others. They were a team, even if Damian was behaving selfishly. And everything that hurt each individual would hurt the team as a whole.

"Stay here," growled Matt. "Don't move a muscle. OK?"

Damian nodded. He looked terrified.

Matt left the room, slamming the door behind him.

He walked quickly to where Judy was posted up by the window that looked out over the front yard.

From down in the basement came the wild cries, somewhat muffled, of the drug-soaked Mia.

"Any sign of him? Or anyone else?" he said to Judy, speaking brusquely.

"No sign of his car," said Judy.

"We've got a problem with your son."

Judy raised her eyebrow quizzically.

Matt found that his heart rate had accelerated and there was a lump in his throat. Anxiety had replaced his anger.

He didn't know how Judy would handle this news about her son.

He knew her, sure, but not that well.

She seemed to have her head on straighter than her son. She seemed practical minded and reasonable, and that was the only reason that he'd confide this to her.

If she'd been any one else, any other mother, he would have had to think of another solution to the situation.

"Talk to me," said Judy.

Matt explained the situation as briefly and succinctly as he could. All the while, he watched Judy's face to see how she would react.

Her face remained completely impassive. She listened carefully to every word, giving no indication of how she would react.

What if she got upset? What if she got angry and called them all a bunch of liars, accused them of attacking her son and threw them all out of the house?

Well, if he hadn't told her, and hadn't done anything about Damian's possible infection, then they'd all wind up dead anyway.

He didn't have a lot to lose.

"Stay here," she said. "Someone needs to watch the window. I'll take care of this."

Gun in hand, she marched off, leaving Matt standing there, wondering what was happening.

Suddenly, someone else rushed into the room. It happened so fast it was hard, for a split second, to tell who it was.

Then he saw that it was Jamie.

"Hey," he said. "We need someone by the front door."

Matt glued his eyes to the window, holding the curtain back just a little.

"If someone comes up now..."

"This is really important," said Jamie. "I had to show you."

She held up her cell phone for him to see. There was a video up and in full-screen mode. She pressed the large play button in the shape of an arrow.

"We really need someone at the door," said Matt, trying to push the cell phone out of the way. "If you're not going to be there, then I'll have to..."

"Seriously," said Jamie, her voice cutting through his. There was a seriousness to her tone. "You *need* to watch this."

Matt gave in.

The first few seconds of the video had been just a blur, as if the lens had been up against someone's shirt, or blocked somehow. But now he could see people moving around.

A lot of people.

There were people everywhere. Too many of them.

It looked like a rock concert.

"What am I looking at?" he said, not taking his eyes off the screen.

"Today. An hour ago. In the convention center."

The people in the video were moving around in a strange way. They were still a little blurry, as if someone had tried to use the digital zoom.

"Keep watching," said Jamie. "The bad stuff is coming."

Matt didn't know what happened in the video, whether the person filming had stepped forward, or whether something else had happened, but he could suddenly see clearly what was happening.

The people, who were crowded together, were writhing around. It almost looked like they were dancing.

They were vomiting. Almost all of them.

Vomiting blood.

There was blood everywhere.

Blood on their faces. On their clothes.

Blood on the floor.

Blood coming from their noses. Their ears.

"Shit," muttered Matt, wanting to take his eyes off the video, but knowing that he needed to keep watching.

The sound on the video, which had for some reason been off, suddenly cut on.

The sound of the vomiting was intense.

There was also the sound of screaming. Horrible screams.

A gunshot. Clearly a gunshot.

The person filming the video spun the camera around, probably about 180 degrees in the other direction.

It was a little hard to see what was happening, but it seemed to be a shot of one of the exits.

There were so many people that it was hard to tell exactly what was preventing the people from leaving, but what *was clear* was that people wanted to get out. But they couldn't.

"I watched it twice," said Jamie. "I think the doors are locked."

It was horrible. The whole scene was disgusting. People were punching each other. Tackling each other. Grabbing each other.

It was chaos. Violent chaos.

There was blood.

Another gunshot off camera.

But the bullet hit someone who was on camera. They collapsed. Then got trampled.

Someone else vomited blood.

"This isn't good," said Matt, completely stunned. "They're all going to die."

"Yes," said Jamie, her voice dead serious. It sounded far away. Sort of hollow. "They are all going to die. Keep watching."

Matt didn't have to be told. Despite the horror, his eyes were glued to the screen.

The camera spun around once again. This time it landed on the cameraman's face. He was holding the phone as if he was going to take a selfie.

His face was sweaty. Distraught. An expression of complete terror on his face.

"If anyone's watching this," he said, having to speak very loudly over the incredible noise in in the background. Occasionally his words were obscured by a gunshot or hideously loud scream. "Please we need... We're all stuck in here in Albuquerque... They won't let us out... We're all going to be infected... Die... My family... Two of us have it already... They were trying to quarantine the infected ones but it wasn't any good... Please, we need the National Guard or something..."

Suddenly, the image went all blurry, as if the camera had been knocked out of his hand.

There was a gunshot.

A scream.

"Did he die?" said Matt. "Wouldn't he have to upload the video afterwards?"

"He was live streaming it," said Jamie. "It was automatically uploaded..."

Matt had been hoping there was some reason to mistrust the video. But he'd seen it all with his own eyes.

The truth was evident.

This was serious.

Very serious.

"If this is what's happening just in Albuquerque," he said. "It means..."

"That the virus is *highly* contagious," said Jamie. "Just like they feared. And this is going to be happening all over the country."

Matt nodded. "It's more important now than ever before that we stay confined to this house," he said. "We can't risk going out..."

"And Damian?"

"His mom's talking to him now."

As if on cue, a high-pitched wail of pain came from the other room.

J udy had taken her son's arm and twisted it around behind his back.

He'd screamed in pain.

"You sound like a girl when you scream," hissed Judy.

She was mad. More mad than she'd been in a long, long time.

"I can't believe you'd do this to us. I can't believe you'd do this to your friends. Forget about doing it to your own mother. What about your friends? You might have killed them all."

There were tears of pain in her son Damian's eyes. "I didn't mean to..."

"Like hell you didn't," hissed Judy. "I don't see how this can be seen as anything but a superbly cowardly act on your part. You wanted to maybe save your own skin, I guess. But that's not even going to work."

"But the virus isn't supposed to be contagious until the veins appear," said Matt, in a pleading voice. "If anything happened, if my veins looked big, then I was going to get out of here quick and let everyone know..."

"Sure you were," hissed Judy. "If you weren't my son, why I'd just..."

She trailed off. She wasn't really sure what she would have done.

Not that it mattered.

He *was* her son.

And he very well might have been infected.

She knew from experience that the anger, in some ways, was a mask for her other emotions. For instance, she was terrified that she'd lose her only son.

It was easier to feel the anger than the fear.

But she was also just furious with him for pulling this stunt.

"OK," she said, suddenly making up her mind, coming up with a plan on the spot. "We don't know exactly how this all works, the vectors of contamination and all that..."

"But they had it all up on the internet," said Damian. "No one's contagious until the veins are enlarged.. I think... It's been a while since I had my phone..."

"You don't even know what you saw," said Judy. "And you're talking about the internet anyway. How often is the internet right? Fifty percent of the time? We just don't know how this virus works... So here's what we're going to do. You're going to stay outside until late tomorrow."

"Outside? You mean out of the house?"

"That's my definition of 'outside,' yes," said Judy coldly. "Here's the situation: Either you've got the virus or you don't. If you have it, then we've either already caught it or we haven't. The only way to make the most of all those possibilities is to keep you outside for a period of over twelve hours. If you're clean, we'll let you back in."

"And what if I have it?"

"Then you'll die," said Judy. It was strange and horrible speaking those words to her own son. But it was the truth. And she wasn't the sort to spin a web of nonsense. "And maybe we'll be dead too, since it you might have already infected us for all we know. Come on, let's get this over with."

"But, mom! You can't just throw me out! There's someone out there who wants to attack us... it's going to be night soon... what will I do?"

"That's your problem," said Judy. "If you'd been upfront with us, we would have set something up for you. We'll do what we can for you. But there isn't much time. Every minute you spend in here, the more likely we are to get infected. Come on."

"Come on, Mom, you can't!"

"You're going to make this tough, aren't you?"

Damian was crying. Just like back when he was a little boy and his toys had broken.

It was tough.

Tough being a mother.

Her hand was still on her gun. She had the muzzle pointed at her son. Her only son.

There were tears in her own eyes. But she managed to bark the commands.

"Get moving," she said. "Don't make this any harder on me. You've made this hard enough already."

He wasn't moving. Just crying.

"Mom, you can't," he begged, sinking down to his knees.

She adjusted the gun's position, jamming the muzzle harder into his soft flesh. "I'm not kidding," she said. "This isn't a joke. This isn't my fault. Every minute that you spend in here puts us all at risk. This is life or death. I have no choice."

She knew she had no choice. She knew that she was doing the right thing. She knew that she was acting rationally. But it didn't make it all any easier.

"You're not going to shoot me," sobbed Damian, clutching at her legs.

"I *will* shoot you, Damian," she said, speaking sternly. "And you know it. Now get up before I *have* to shoot you."

He looked up at her, saw her face, and knew she was telling the truth.

He stood up, and she walked behind him, the gun not leaving her hand as he shuffled through the house.

"Back door," she said.

He took a turn, shuffling towards the back door.

"You're not to come within ten feet of the house," she said. "I suggest you spend the night in the shed," referring to the shed in the back corner of the yard.

"But, Mom!"

"If you come too close to the house, we're going to have no choice. We'll have to shoot you."

"Mom!"

He was crying now. Huge tears running down his cheeks. It was horrible to see. And horrible to have to be in Judy's position. But she had no choice. It wasn't just her own life she had to think about. It was the others. What kind of person would she be if she gave her son the ultimate pass and let him infect others who had a chance to live?

"Open the door."

"Mom!"

"Open it."

He opened the door.

"Outside," she said. It was clearly an order. There was no other way to interpret her tone.

She had the gun in her hand.

She'd use it if she had to.

She knew she was doing the right thing. Sometimes the right thing was the hard thing. The seemingly impossible thing.

He stepped out the door.

"Remember: ten feet."

She slammed the door shut behind him. Locked it. Deadbolt and everything.

It was all over.

She breathed out a sigh of relief.

She still felt the anger. The anger that had allowed her to act, allowed her to do the right thing.

The anger was real. She felt it because her son had put her in this position. He was the one who'd done this. Not her.

She watched her son through the window. He stood for a long, long moment, and for a second she worried that he wasn't going to leave the stoop.

But he did. He didn't look back. He walked slowly across the yard towards the shed.

He opened the door and disappeared into the shed, closing the door behind him.

There was one small window in that shed. There'd be a little light in there for him.

Hopefully he'd be OK. He'd acted horribly. He'd acted irresponsibly. It was definitely the most irresponsible thing she'd ever known him to do. She thought she'd raised him better.

Judy watched to make sure that Damian didn't just immediately open the shed door and try to do something stupid.

Now that he was in there, it seemed likely he'd stay there inside there, sulking by himself.

She made her way back through the house.

"How'd it go?" said Matt, at the window.

"As well as it could."

"I heard most of it."

Judy filled him in on the details. "I figure he can stay out there until at least noon tomorrow... by then we'll know whether he was infected."

"And whether we were," said Matt, holding up the back of his hand. "How do they look?"

"The veins? Normal. Any sign of our friend outside?"

"The dead man's friend? No. He's either fled or he's waiting for a more opportune moment."

"Like nightfall."

"Exactly what I was thinking. If I were him, and I wanted revenge, I'd wait until night. I've got the door jammed up here pretty good. Hope you don't have a problem with us using your furniture like this, but we needed more than just the dining room table."

He was leading the way into the other room where Jamie stood by the door. There was a pile of furniture pushed up against it.

"I always knew there was a reason to have all that heavy furniture," said Judy, trying to defuse the sadness of the situation with her son with a joke.

Matt and Jamie didn't seem to understand that it was a joke, and the conversation just moved along.

"I figure we'll need to take shifts throughout the night," said Matt. "People are going to need to rest."

"I think Mia's already fallen asleep."

"Yeah, her screams died down."

"I put my ear to the door and I was pretty sure I heard some loud snores."

"She snores?"

"Like crazy. Every night..." As she said this, Jamie's eyes glanced up at Judy.

Maybe Judy was wrong, but it seemed like Jamie had caught herself starting to tell some sort of joke about her roommate and then had decided that it wasn't appropriate given the fact that Judy had just had to force her son at gunpoint out of the house.

"Maybe she'll be sober when she wakes up," said Matt.

"I hope so," said Judy. "Now that my loser son's not here, it's just the three of us now. We could use a fourth. Especially for the watch shifts. How do you want break it down?"

"I'll take first shift," said Matt. He glanced at his watch. "What do you say? Six hours on?"

"Just one person on shift?"

"If we have two people awake at at time, it means we're all going to be more tired. And we have no idea what kind of challenges tomorrow will throw at us."

"You're right," said Judy. "We need to be well rested."

"I'm going to check the window again," said Matt abruptly.

He left the room, disappearing around a corner.

It was starting to get dark outside. The sun was sinking down, and the light was fading.

It'd be dark in half an hour. Maybe less.

It had reached that point where it was about to get hard to see indoors.

"Here, Judy, let me show you this," said Jamie, pulling out a phone. "You've got to see this. I showed Matt the video and it's just crazy."

"I hope that's some kind of young people slang for

'everything's going fine and the authorities have figured out the virus.'"

Jamie shook her head. "I wish," she said. "No, it's bad. In the convention center... well, you just have to watch it..."

Jamie tapped at her phones screen and held it up so that Judy could see it.

But nothing happened.

"It's not playing," said Judy.

"Here, just a second. Let me get this..."

Jamie took the phone and started tapping at it.

"What's wrong?"

"It's weird... Let me reload this page... It's strange because it's like loading and then it won't play..."

"Has it ever done that before?"

Jamie shook her head. "Not that I can remember. Shit, yeah, it's just not going to play."

Jamie explained what was in the video.

"I can't say I'm surprised, as horrific as it is."

"All those people are as good as dead."

Judy nodded. "And I think we've got another problem on our hands. Maybe one that's more severe."

"What's more severe than that? Than all those people dying?"

"The fact that the social media networks are apparently going down."

"Why do you say that? Let me check another one..."

A moment later, Judy was muttering to herself.

"It's not working, right?"

"No, it's not."

"And this doesn't happen?"

"It just can't be down," said Jamie. "It just can't. How are we going to know what's happening?"

"The old-fashioned way," said Judy.

But Jamie didn't seem to hear her. Her eyes were glued to her phone. Her fingers were tapping away at the screen. But nothing seemed to be working. And it was evident from her cursing and muttering that none of the normal sites were working. Not just the social media sites. But also none of the internet sites.

"It's really weird. It seems like I can get online, but then the pages just don't load all the way now... And it's getting worse..."

"They must be overloaded," said Judy. "Either that or the people who maintain the networks are getting sick."

Judy didn't know much about technology, especially not the internet. But it was just common sense, as far as she could see.

"Guys!" shouted Matt, from the other room. "We've got a problem!"

19

MATT

"What is it?"

Judy came rushing into the room.

It was almost completely dark now

They hadn't turned on any of the lights in the house, and Matt's eyes were adjusting to the growing darkness, so he could still see fairly well.

But not as well as when the sun had been up.

"People in the street," he said.

"Where? I don't see them?"

"Come over here. Let me move out of the way for you. They're down at the end of the block."

They switched positions, and Judy peered out the window for a long moment before she said, "yeah, I see them now. Three of them?"

"That's what it looks like to me," said Matt.

"You think we should be concerned?"

"Let me put it this way," said Matt. "I don't think you can see it now, but earlier I saw that one on the end carrying what looked like a baseball bat."

"You sure?"

Matt nodded.

"What do we do?"

"Wait it out."

"What about the front door?"

"It should look OK from the outside. We've got more furniture behind it. It should hold up. If they break through, we shoot them."

"Let's not get ahead of ourselves."

"Who's getting ahead of ourselves? We're just planning."

Matt continued to watch the group of people out in the street. A minute passed, then another. Then another.

The people looked like they were adults. Hard to tell if they were men or women. But they were probably men, just judging by their size.

The men in the street didn't seem to be doing much at all. Just milling around. Standing there.

Matt glanced at his watch. Fifteen minutes had passed. Hardly anyone had spoken, and the group of men at the end of the street had barely moved.

Slowly, Matt's accelerated pulse had started to die back down. Slowly, he realized that he felt calmer.

What were the chances that the men in the street would attack them? Probably not too great.

After all, what did attacking an occupied house have to offer anyone? Just danger.

Well, that and supplies. Food. Water. Things that might soon become quite scarce.

There were too many angles to this whole thing, this whole situation. Too many ways to think about it all. Too many things that could go wrong.

There were, it seemed, a thousand different ways to die.

After all, they might already be infected. They might already be dead.

He needed to just focus on the here and now. Worry about what was in front of him.

The sun had now set, and the figures in the street quickly became shadows.

The street lights came on and the shadows became harder to see with less light behind them.

But Matt found that if he kept his eyes on them, he could still see the figures, shifting here and there, pacing back and forth. Not doing much at all. But they were there. They were still a threat.

Nearby, Judy and Jamie were talking about what it meant that the social media sites were apparently down.

To Matt, it meant that things were starting to fall apart.

The whole system, he thought, would soon come crashing down.

How much longer would the electricity work for?

"You two had better get some sleep," said Matt. "Talking about the internet isn't going to make it come back online."

"It's so early though," said Jamie.

"Check on Mia before you bed down," said Matt. "Make sure she hasn't hurt herself."

"OK, but I'm not tired though."

"I bet you're more tired than you realize. I'm going to be waking you up at about three in the morning. So you'd better get some sleep while you can. This isn't going to work unless we stick to a good schedule."

"All right," grumbled Jamie.

Matt heard Jamie's and Judy's footsteps as they walked through the house, heading to the basement door, and eventually heading upstairs.

It got darker and Matt was left to his own thoughts. Silence surrounded him now.

There was still the distant hum of the city in the

distance, but it was so much a part of what he was used to that he barely noticed it.

The people in the street made no noise, and there wasn't a peep out of Mia in the basement, nor from Damian who was apparently still in the shed. Nor from the man who'd driven away.

And last but not least, there was, of course, no sound from the corpse on the front stoop.

Maybe the bloodied corpse would serve as a warning to others who might dare to do the same thing.

Or maybe it might attract trouble. After all, someone else might think that if someone had died trying to get into the house, then it might be worth the trouble to try themselves. Maybe the dead guy knew something.

The darkness grew around Matt. He'd told Judy and Jamie not to turn on any lights. He didn't want to attract any more attention than necessary.

The men in the street had likely already seen the corpse on the front stoop, but hopefully it'd be invisible to anyone else who happened by.

Matt glanced at his watch occasionally. The minutes turned into hours and the hours ticked by.

Before he knew it, it was already 10:00 p.m. And nothing had happened. Absolutely nothing.

He'd glanced down at his phone a couple times, trying to see if the internet would work again. But no luck. Every site seemed down.

By merely glancing down at his phone, he'd messed up his adaptive night vision.

So when he looked back at the street through the window, he could no longer see the shadowy figures. They were invisible despite the street lights not so far away.

But he had to assume that they were still there.

"Psst, hey, it's just me." A soft female voice came wafting towards him in the darkness.

"Jamie?" he said.

"Yeah. It's me. Didn't want to scare you."

"Good call. What's up?"

"Couldn't sleep."

He heard her moving towards him in the darkness.

He grunted vaguely.

"Anything going on out here?"

"Nope," he said. "And the internet still seems to be down. Hey, while you're up, why don't you try their home computer? Maybe it's just the cell networks that are down."

"Already tried it," said Jamie, speaking like Matt in a low whisper-like voice that seemed appropriate for the darkness. "Judy had a computer upstairs. I got on it. It turned on and everything, and their home router worked, but no sites will load. Which means that the internet service provider isn't working... it's overloaded..."

"So it could just be a local issue?"

"I don't know. Given that our cell phones aren't connecting, I'd say it's a larger issue. Probably national."

"Shit. That's not good."

"No, it's not. Did you try the radio or TV or anything?"

"Nope," said Matt. "I've been staring out the window the whole time."

"I'll go try them."

She let him alone in the darkness, returning less than ten minutes later.

"Bad news," she muttered.

"What is it?"

"Well, there are no channels coming in on the TV. No stations on the radio."

"None at all? You try everything?"

"Yeah. Everything."

"Shit. That's really not good."

"What does it mean? How are all the radio stations down?"

"You didn't even find a single one?"

"No," she said. "What does it mean?"

"I think it means more people are infected than we would have thought."

"You mean that everybody who's been working at the stations is now dead from the infection?"

"Well, either that, or they couldn't get to work. Or the people who somehow kept the stations pumping the signal out into our area... they couldn't get to work. It's not that far-fetched if you consider the video from the convention center... think about how many people are going to be stuck inside there, or stuck in traffic somewhere, or stuck at work..."

"Or already dead from the virus," she said, finishing his thought for him.

"Yeah. Or that. Definitely possible. It seems like the timeline they presented on TV was wrong. At least for some people."

"So you think that's what's going on with the internet? The TV?"

"Probably."

"So how are we going to have any clue what's going on? It's seems impossible... we don't have any news of the outside world. Here we are in the middle of a large city and we're completely cut off from the outside world..."

"I think we already have our news," said Matt.

"What do you mean?"

"The fact that none of it works... that there are no TV

stations... that's our news right there... it's all we need to know."

"Hey," said Jamie. "Something looks different outside..."

She had pulled the curtain back where she was and had her face pressed against the glass.

Matt, who'd been looking towards her direction in the darkness, looked back out the window.

He immediately spotted what the difference was.

The street lights had gone out.

Completely out.

It was darker than it had been before. Much darker.

"The street lights are out," he said.

"Shit," she said. "That's what it is, isn't it? It's so dark. I can hardly see anything."

"It gets worse."

"What? How? You see something else?"

Matt didn't answer her. Instead, he stood up.

He had a hunch. But he didn't want to be right.

He walked across the room, using his flashlight to light up the way.

His hand found a lamp. Found the switch. Flipped it.

Nothing.

Nothing happened.

"The power's out," he said.

"No way," she said. "Maybe it's just that lamp."

"And the street lights?"

"Let me try one."

He heard her getting up, walking across the room.

He heard the flipping of a switch. One of those switches that are built into the power cord.

Nothing. No light came on.

"Shit," she was muttering. "The power can't be out... it just can't be..."

"It makes sense, though," said Matt. "If the radio stations are all dead... if the internet servers are down... if there's no one left to mange those, then who's going to be running the power grid and the power plants?"

"But it can't be..."

She cut herself off, and there was a tremendous crashing sound in the darkness.

Evidently, Jamie had fallen.

"You OK?" he said.

"...Yeah," she said, after a pause.

Matt found her with his flashlight's beam.

She'd walked into a table and now lay on the floor.

"Let me help you up."

He reached down and pulled her to her feet. She seemed to be limping a little, and it was a little awkward getting her to her feet.

"Thanks," she said, losing her balance a little, her body fell against his body, as if they were hugging.

It was strange. The last time they'd been that close, they'd been on a date.

He was about to say something. Maybe make a joke. Try to defuse the tension that seemed to hang in the area.

But before he could, she screamed.

A piercing scream.

"What?" he yelled.

He swung his flashlight around, turning his head along with it.

Then he saw it.

At the window, where the curtain was pulled back, there was a face.

A human face pressed against the glass. The features were distorted, smushed against the window pane.

But it wasn't hard to tell who it was.

It was Damian.

Damian was holding one of those plastic lanterns that people buy for camping. He was holding it right next to his face.

His mouth was open. Was it a grin? Was it something else? It was disturbing, whatever the expression was.

Now he was mouthing something. Mouthing some words that they couldn't hear.

"He's infected," came Jamie's words, much softer than her scream.

It was true.

Easy to see. Easy to spot.

Damian's neck was pressed against the glass. One the side, there was a single huge bulging vein. It was unmistakable.

Suddenly, Damian slammed his closed fist into the window. It made a tremendous noise. The glass shook.

"What do we do?" said Jamie.

Matt's hand was already on his gun. He was pulling it from its holster.

He had his Glock in one hand. Flashlight in the other.

He kept his flashlight trained on Damian on the other side of the window.

"Get my mom!" shouted Damian, his words suddenly audible through the glass. Maybe he'd just been moving his mouth before, or maybe he was raising his voice now.

"What should we do?"

"Get her!" shouted Jamie, as Damian's fist slammed again and again into the glass.

There was a good chance that he'd break the glass.

"Get Judy," said Matt.

He didn't take his flashlight off of Damian, and he didn't

take his hand off his Glock, which he kept pointed at Damian.

If Damian got inside, there was a good chance he'd infect everyone.

If they weren't already infected, that is.

20

DAMIAN

D amian had spent what had felt like an eternity sitting alone in that shed, wondering if he was going to die or not.

A little light had come in through the dirty window, and he'd used it to frantically check his veins. Both his neck and the back of his hands.

For a long time, everything had seemed normal. It had seemed as if he hadn't been infected.

He hadn't had his phone to occupy himself, so his mind was left to wander. And to obsess.

He obsessed about how unfair it all was. How unjust.

How could his own mother treat him like that? How could she point a gun at her own flesh and blood?

She'd given birth to him. She'd brought him into the world. And now she was willing to take him out of it?

He'd noticed the enlarged veins right before the sun had gone down. He's seen the back of his hands, felt a sinking feeling in his stomach, and realized that he was going to die.

He visualized the whole thing in graphic detail. He imagined blood erupting from his various orifices. He imagined the pain that he'd feel, and he imagined just what he would look like from another person's perspective.

And he knew how it would happen. He'd be out there, alone in the yard.

There was no way they'd let him inside. There'd be no way to hide the fact that he was infected.

His anger only grew as he thought about it all.

What a way to end. Out in the cold on his own. At night.

He'd be dead before morning. He'd already seen the sun for the last time.

That was it.

It was all over.

He'd never been the sort of man who'd thought much about death. His attitude had been avoidant. Now confronted with the reality that this was it, that he'd lived all he was going to live, he was shot through with fear and rage.

Rage at how unjust his whole life had been.

Suddenly, his ruminations took on a different tone and he fixated on the countless injustices that had befallen him through his life.

"It's just not fair," he found himself muttering alone in the darkness. "They think they're just going to let me die out here... my own mother... my friend... I mean, come on. Is this what I'm really worth to them? My mother's going to let them stay in my house? And me? Out here on my own. Dangerous people all around."

That's when he'd decided to leave the shed.

He didn't bother closing the door behind him. He just left it opened.

Even to his darkness-adjusted eyes, looking back at the shed was somehow a terrifying sight. The door frame seemed to yawn open to a chasm as dark as anything had ever been.

He snuck around the side of the house. His footsteps were light.

"Starting to feel kind of weird," he muttered to himself. "Yup. Kind of weird. Maybe it's just the worry though. The anxiety of what's to come."

He had a battery-powered lantern with him that he'd found in the shed.

In his other hand, he carried an old rusty shovel. It had a pointed end. It would make a good weapon. If he needed one.

And he might.

He held the lantern in front of him as he walked.

Up ahead, he could see the bloodied corpse on the front stoop.

The throat was all opened up.

It was a horrible body. A horrible sight. Lying right there on the steps that he used to play on as a child.

"What's the world coming to?"

He glanced at the window.

No lights on.

Turning towards the street, the yellowish glow of the streetlights looked pleasant.

Almost like some bug attracted to light, he found himself walking and shuffling towards the street.

That body on the steps? That would be him. Soon enough.

His thoughts were getting jumbled. A little confused.

Was it hunger? Was it exhaustion? Was it the stress?

Was it the infection itself?

Soon enough, he'd be hemorrhaging. Surely, his brain couldn't be working that well.

He probably already had a fever.

In fact, was that sweat on his forehead? Beads of sweat? Wasn't his hair too damp, especially for the cool night air?

There seemed to be some people milling around down on one end of the street, out of the glow of the streetlights. But he couldn't be sure. It seemed that when he looked at them, they just disappeared.

Why could he only see them out of the corner of his eye?

Maybe they were just figments of his imagination.

But were they making noise? Sort of like low murmurs?

Maybe. He didn't know.

It spooked him.

He didn't want to spend his last hours on Earth spooked, so he walked the other direction. Away from them.

What was he going to do?

Why was he headed down the street?

What he really wanted to do was die near his mother. But she wouldn't let him in.

She wouldn't let him in.

The words rang through his head.

"She's not going to let me in," he found himself saying, over and over again.

"What's that, friend?" a silky male voice came oozing out of the darkness.

Damian stopped dead in his tracks.

But he found that he wasn't scared.

His heart didn't start racing.

Adrenaline didn't start pumping.

After all, what did he have to be scared of? He had already sunk deep down into the depression that came with imminent death. What more could anyone do to him? Take away his last few hours? It didn't matter that much.

"Who's there?" said Damian, his voice only very vaguely curious.

"Just a friend."

Damian was peering through the darkness, holding his lantern. But he saw no one.

Then he realized who it was.

"Oh," he said, sounding kind of bored. "You're that guy from earlier... the friend of the dead guy."

"You caught me."

The creaking sound of a car door.

A couple footsteps in the silence.

Suddenly, the street lights went off.

Everything fell into darkness.

Complete darkness. Except for the battery-powered camping lantern. Which didn't give off much light.

Silence too. A lot of silence. Maybe more that he'd ever heard. It was as if every piece of machinery for miles and miles was powering down.

"It's happening," said the male voice. Still sounded silky. Reminded Damian of a snake.

The man stepped into the dim light of the lantern.

He had greasy hair. A disgusting face, in many ways.

Damian almost started to say, "stay back," and to threaten him with the shovel, but he found that he just didn't have the energy for it. He found that he just didn't care.

Imminent death had taken it all away from him. Motivation. Everything.

"You're from the house, aren't you?" said the man, his face scrunching up in a strange way when he spoke.

"Yeah," said Damian. "Was that your friend there on the steps?"

"Yeah. Did you shoot him?"

"No. My friend did. And before you get upset, there's no point in killing me. I'm already infected."

"Infected? You don't believe in all that, do you?"

"What's there not to believe in? It's a virus. It's killing people. Look at my hands."

"The veins? So what? I've got that too."

The man held up his wrists. In the darkness, it was clear that he was infected too.

"You've got it too. Don't you realize that? You're going to die."

"Die?" The man laughed. "They're always going on about some virus... Every year it seems... and when does it happen? When does it kill everyone? We're going to be fine. Come on. The veins don't mean anything... Why are you out here anyway? Why aren't you inside?"

"They kicked me out. They're worried I'm going to infect them all. My own mother. She kicked me out."

"Your own mother? That's cold, man. Real cold. Ice cold. She can't do that to you."

"I guess she has her reasons. They say I'm going to kill them all. I didn't tell them I was infected, you see."

More laughter. "But there's no such thing as this being infected. It's all some ruse. Some trick. Just more garbage from the media. It's all the same. And now they've kicked you out of what's got to be your own house. How is that cool? It's not."

"How can you be so sure it's not real? The virus, I mean?"

Damian found himself interested in the possibility. After all, if it wasn't real, he wouldn't die. That reasoning in and of itself was a pretty strong pull. It carried a lot of weight.

Damian knew that people could convince themselves of just about anything, so long as it sounded appealing to them.

But that didn't mean that he wasn't prey to the same thing himself.

As he listened to this stranger talking, and even ranting, he found himself believing every word of it.

"Yeah," said Damian. "I bet you're right. You know what? This is all a big scam. All that stuff in the news? They just put that there to get us all riled up. What? I'm going to die because my veins are a little bigger? That just doesn't make sense. Maybe I've got something. Maybe a little cold. Maybe it is a virus from China."

"But that doesn't mean that you're going to die, right?" said the stranger enthusiastically.

"No!" cried Damian, throwing his fist with the lantern clutched in it into the air. "No way!"

"Of course," said the man, somewhat more soberly. "This doesn't mean that you're not going to get hurt out here."

"Hurt out here?" said Damian, his joy and excitement instantly draining from him. "What are you talking about?"

"The media has gotten everyone riled up. That makes this all very dangerous. Bandits and crazy people are going to be roving the streets... look at what happened in your own front yard. Right?"

"Huh, I guess, yeah..."

"They've sentenced you to death," he said. "By throwing you out in the street... you're as good as dead... why don't they just put a bullet in your head themselves?"

"Shit... I never thought about it that way."

Damian felt shaken up.

He was completely convinced that this man was right.

His own mother had sentenced him to death! It was all worse than he'd thought. Much worse.

"What should I do?"

"You've got to get back in that house. Any way you can. No matter what. That's the only way you're going to be safe."

"Get back in the house?"

"Yeah. Do whatever you have to do. You're going to get killed by some criminals out here... it's just not safe."

Damian felt confused. It felt as if he still had a fever.

But it was good to know that he had a chance.

All he had to do was get back into his mother's house.

Muttering to himself, he turned around and started marching down the darkened street, towards the house.

For a while, it sounded like the man was following him. He could hear footsteps on the pavement.

But when he turned around, there was no one there.

Whatever. It wasn't Damian's problem.

He was going to do whatever it took.

Even if it meant hurting his friends.

They'd betrayed him.

They'd bought into all this bullshit.

So he'd betray them. If he had to.

Why was it so hot?

There was a funny taste in his mouth.

He wiped the back of his sleeve against his forehead. It came back drenched. Completely drenched in sweat.

Probably just because he was nervous.

Chaz wasn't dumb enough to pass up an opportunity. Not when it was staring him in the face.

He'd been dumb enough to find himself in jail for the last ten years. But that hadn't really been his fault. The only thing he'd done wrong was trust the wrong woman.

She'd turned him in. Something that he'd never forget. It had changed his life.

He'd been a successful small-time drug dealer. He hadn't made a killing, but he hadn't necessarily wanted to. After all, those were the guys who took the hits. The guys who made the big bucks were the guys who went to jail.

And Chaz had wanted to stay out of jail.

He'd made a comfortable living. Enough to buy a house. A car. A regular car, nothing super fancy.

He'd made enough to support his woman. He'd bought her a car. Clothes. Jewelry. Nothing too crazy. Just enough to keep her happy. Just enough to keep her at his side.

She was a looker. She knew it. Chaz knew it.

Everything had been going great. Better than great. Chaz

had managed to avoid doing the thing that he'd hated in this world above all else, which was work.

Chaz considered work to be the greatest evil of all.

The way he saw it, his small-time drug dealing wasn't really work. It was mostly hanging out with friends. Slinging a few pills here and there. Nothing crazy. Nothing too demanding. Nothing that required him to break a sweat.

So when his woman had betrayed him, it had been a huge hit.

He'd stood no chance during the trial. She'd even testified against him.

He'd gone to jail, where he'd stayed for ten years.

He'd spent the first year moping around, wondering how his woman could have screwed him over like that.

Then he'd gotten a hold of himself and started to come back from it. He'd built up his body. He'd filled pillowcases with heavy things and lifted them over his head thousands of times. He'd figured out how to do every type of push-up imaginable. He'd done pull-ups on the bunk bed.

Contrary to popular belief, every type of substance and drug was usually freely available in prison. For a price.

He'd found a good supplier of steroids and loaded up. He'd be shooting himself up with testosterone before breakfast, lunch and dinner.

He'd gotten huge. Lean. And muscular.

He'd started commanding respect. A lot of respect.

It had been gradual. And it had been a struggle.

But he'd made a name for himself. He was known as a fair man. But a man that took what he needed and didn't hesitate to exact his revenge.

He was respected and feared in the prison. Which is just how it should have been. It's what he deserved.

He'd spent years finding his place. He'd spent years taking what he deserved.

So when the virus had come, and when he'd understood what was happening, he almost lamented it all.

After all, he recognized that the virus meant the end of his prison life. It meant the end of the power that he'd earned there.

At first, he'd resisted.

He'd watched the news on TV in the rec room with the other inmates. He'd understood how serious this all was.

He'd watched as a guard had gotten sick out on the yard. He'd seen how his veins had been big. Huge, even. He'd watched from a safe distance as the guard had started hemorrhaging, blood spewing everywhere as he spasmed on the concrete like an epileptic.

Chaz had known then and there that his life in prison was over. He'd been absolutely sure.

And soon enough, there were prisoners sick. It wasn't just the guard. Ten men. Then twenty men. All with enlarged veins. Then two more guards.

The end of it all had actually been anticlimatic. Boring. Even trivial.

Many of the guards had simply not come into work.

The security in the prison had always been suspect. The inmates had long known the weak points.

It hadn't been hard for them to break out.

It was a mass breakout. The first in a long, long time. Chaz didn't know of one before.

It had been then that he'd decided he wasn't going out in the world, which was in many ways totally new to him, without a gang of strong dependable men around him.

He wasn't going to go back to being the little guy. He didn't want to once again be in the position that he'd been in when he'd been just small-time. Back then, his woman had been able to betray him, completely without consequences.

In prison, he'd gotten himself to where that simply wasn't possible. No one could betray him on the inside without consequence.

And now?

Now he needed men.

Fortunately, his reputation served him well. As did the fear that the men felt.

There were many who'd been locked up since they were teenagers. Kids, even.

Some of them had been in and out of juvie, and then in and out of prison. The same pattern over and over until the convictions had piled up enough to put them away for decades.

There were men who were terrified of life on the outside of the prison walls.

But they'd never admit it.

They'd needed a leader.

Chaz had understood them. He'd understood how to manipulate them.

It hadn't taken that much. A couple rousing speeches. A few promises of women and riches. And that was about it.

It had almost been too easy.

And now?

Now he found himself standing on a residential street in Albuquerque, surrounding by ten strong men, all of whom were dependable enough that they'd die for him. All of them looked up to him almost like a father figure. They'd do anything he wanted.

They were strong men. They could accomplish a lot.

But what Chaz relished was the feeling of control. The feeling of being the puppet master. The feeling of being the one who could take a man's life with nothing more than a word. Nothing more than a command.

They had no guns.

But they had other weapons.

Baseball bats. Crowbars. Sticks.

They could do a lot of damage with what they had.

And more important than the weapons were the drugs.

Everyone except Chaz was high on something. Or multiple things.

Chaz knew about "not getting high on your own supply." It was the cardinal rule for successful drug dealers, the rule that everyone invariably broke.

Everyone except Chaz.

He didn't get high at all. He despised drugs, seeing them only as a vehicle to gain money, respect, and power. He saw them as a tool. A tool of control.

He'd "smoke them all up." He'd given the ones who liked opiates their pills. He'd given others shots of morphine. He'd given the crankheads their fixes, freebase or otherwise.

He'd had access to it all in prison and he'd distributed it freely now.

"Hey, Chaz," said one of them.

Chaz could barely see him in the darkness. The streetlights had gone out minutes earlier.

The hum of the city had died down.

The power was out. Cut off.

Chaz didn't know why. But it didn't matter that much whether or not he knew the specifics.

He understood things in larger ways. Gross, crude ways.

He understood that the city would be in turmoil. He understood that it offered him an opportunity.

He didn't exactly know what the future held. How could he?

But he knew where he wanted to be.

Which was in power.

"Chaz," said the man again.

"What is it?"

"Dan-man is sick with something..."

"What's he got?"

"He looks kind of like those guards who went down in the yard... it's kind of freaky. His veins are huge... He's looking weird in the face... I mean I'm not trying to be a snitch or anything like that, but..."

"No, don't worry. You did the right thing coming to me. Where is he?"

"Over there. Away from the others."

"I'll take care of this. Here, give the guys another few joints. We're going to move on out soon."

The man took the joints greedily. Even in the darkness, the excitement was written pathetically all over his face.

"Hey, Dan-man," said Chaz, speaking in his low rumbly voice, the one that he'd perfected as his "leader voice" over the years. "Can I talk to you for a second?"

The other men parted, letting Chaz through.

They liked Dan-man, who had always been popular and well liked, but Chaz knew that they wouldn't do anything to interfere. They were Chaz's men, not Dan-man's men.

"What's up, boss?" said Dan-man, who was doubled over, his hands on his knees. He didn't sound good. He sounded sick.

"Word is that you're sick."

"It's nothing. Just a cold. Hell, I've been locked up since I was twelve. Triple homicide, you know? Juvie couldn't contain me... my body's just not used to being on the outside..."

"Too much fresh air, eh?" said Chaz, chuckling.

"You know how it is," said Dan-man, his own laughter punctuated with fits of coughing.

"I'm going to have to let you go," said Chaz, speaking quietly.

Chaz knew that everyone was listening. And waiting. And watching.

"Chaz... you can't!" Dan-man's voice was pathetic. Whining.

"I can't let you infect the rest of us... you should have done this yourself... I thought you were one of us... but you're nothing but scum..."

Chaz didn't hide his anger now. He let it shine through his voice.

Chaz had his metal baseball bat in hand. He brought it back, as if he were on the mound.

Then he swung.

A good swing. Really drove his hips into it. His whole body working behind the bat.

Dan-man didn't even bring his hands up. He was already too far gone. Too sick.

The bat connected with Dan-man's face.

Connected hard.

The impact felt good. The shock to Chaz's hands felt good.

Dan-man screamed. A pathetic scream.

Chaz brought the bat back.

Swung again.

And again.

And again.

Dan-man was on the ground. Blood on his face. Blood and bone on the bat.

Chaz turned around, bat hanging in one hand.

"If anyone else is sick, I expect them to take care of it

themselves. We don't have time for stragglers. Only the strong will survive."

No one said a word. No one made a noise.

"Now," continued Chaz. "The bitch who turned me in years ago to the cops... she was living in this house along with her sorority sisters... she might have moved on, but whoever is living there is bound to know their whereabouts..."

Still silence.

Pure silence. It sounded good. It sounded like absolute obedience.

"After I take care of her, the world is ours," said Chaz. "There are no limits now. We're out, and we're not going back in."

These final words were met with a cheer.

Chaz raised his bloodied bat high into the air.

And he knew that these men would do whatever for him.

And he knew that he'd make that bitch who'd turned him in pay.

22

That guy he'd met in the darkness had been a sucker of the first class. And he'd played right into Froggy's hand.

Sure, Froggy didn't believe in this virus garbage. So that part was true.

But he'd told that sucker the rest of it all just so that he'd go cause a distraction. A distraction that Froggy could take advantage of.

Froggy had followed that sucker back to his house. He'd watched as the sucker had started to cause a huge commotion at the window, shining his lantern into the house, making faces in the window, screaming and begging for his mommy.

It had been perfect. Beyond perfect.

There'd been some kind of sound in the street as Froggy crept silently around the side of the house. It had sounded like the crowd cheering at a baseball game.

Whatever. It didn't matter. Froggy just ignored it.

His plan was simple.

While the sucker distracted his family from the front, Froggy would sneak around the back of the house. He'd break in through a window, then creep through the house executing everyone one by one.

That's what they got for killing Mark.

And that's the way Mark would have wanted it.

"I'm doing it all for you, buddy," whispered Froggy to himself and to the dark night.

Froggy got around the back of the house.

It was a little hard to search without a flashlight. After all, it was very dark.

But his eyes were adjusting.

And there was plenty of commotion from the front. He didn't have to worry about getting caught. He could poke around with impunity.

By feeling around, he eventually discovered that there was a back door. But it was locked. And it was made of steel. And it seemed to have a study frame. Too hard to break down.

There were a couple of windows within reach. But they were small. And the glass was sturdy. Froggy knew from experience that some window panes, especially when small, were deceptively difficult to shatter.

And what about getting through a small window like that? Maybe he could do it. But he might cut himself up pretty badly in the process.

And that's when Froggy discovered the door to the basement.

It was locked, sure.

But the lock was flimsy. Typical of basement doors.

He had it open in about five seconds flat. Just a matter of prying it open with a folding knife.

Froggy folded the knife back up and stuffed it into the front pocket of his jeans as he opened the metal basement doors and descended the concrete stairs into the basement.

He had his gun in one hand, wishing he had a flashlight in the other.

But while he expected to find darkness, instead, when he reached the bottom of the stairs, he saw light dancing across the concrete wall.

The light suddenly stopped moving.

"Who's there?" said a voice. A female voice.

Something about her voice sounded strange.

But it also sounded attractive. Youthful. Full of life.

The light left the opposite wall, moving so that now it shone directly onto Froggy.

It was bright. He shielded his eyes.

"You're not... one of them, are you?" said the voice.

"Of course not," said Froggy.

"Good, because I wasn't sure... I have to keep it all a secret... they put me down here.. don't realize what's happening... what it all means..."

Froggy knew a drugged-out voice when he heard one. He had plenty of personal experience. Despite his own strong buzz, he knew how to play right along with it.

"The others sent me," said Froggy. "The others told me to help you."

"The others...?" she said, her voice trailing off. But she sounded somewhat hopeful.

"That's right. Now let me see you. Shine the light on yourself... I have to make sure you're the one I'm supposed to help..."

She obeyed almost immediately, taking the flashlight and shining it on her face.

It was a nice face.

Pretty.

Long hair.

Good features.

Just the type of face that Froggy liked.

Maybe this little raid of his would go better than he'd even expected. He'd been merely hoping to murder everyone here.

But maybe it was time to have some fun.

"Good," said Froggy, licking his lips. "Your face is right. But what about your body? The others told me that I need to check to make sure that you have the right body."

She obeyed, shining the light on her legs, arms, stomach, and chest.

It looked good. It was quite a nice body. The kind of body that Froggy liked.

He licked his lips eagerly as he approached her.

Upstairs, there were heavy footsteps. People running.

Then a yell from upstairs.

Good. The distraction was doing his job at the front of the house. Maybe the guy would even kill some of them for Froggy. Make his job a little easier.

"Hey," she said suddenly, shining the light back on Froggy. "You're one of them!"

"No, no. I'm from the others."

She seemed too messed up on something that she'd believe just about anything. He'd been there himself.

"No. You're going to hurt me. I can see it in your eyes."

Maybe she was starting to sober up.

She started shining the light around wildly, as if it were dancing around the basement.

Froggy was able to see that the basement had been destroyed. It was crowded. Horribly crowded.

And it was as if someone had gone around and taken everything off the shelves and thrown it all on the floor.

"See this?" she said, grabbing a handful of rice grains from the floor. She shone the flashlight right on them, and he watched as they fell from her fist. "See this? This is what I am now. This is my soul."

"You're higher than I thought," whispered Froggy. He was close to her now. He stepped over a knocked-over shelving unit and took another step towards her. "Why don't we have some fun, baby?"

"Get away from me!"

All of a sudden, something smashed into Froggy's head.

Something heavy.

She'd done it.

He hadn't seen it coming at him in the darkness.

She'd smacked him with a heavy sack. Maybe of rice.

"Shit," yelled Froggy, grabbing the side of his head.

It hurt. Like a splitting migraine. The pain flared through his skull.

He didn't need this. He didn't want to put up with this garbage.

Screw having fun. He wasn't in the mood any longer.

He'd just stick to his original plan. Revenge. Murder. Steal a few valuables. All in Mark's memory. Then he'd split.

The flashlight beam was dancing crazily around.

The crazy woman in front of him was chanting. Some kind of crazy shit. Who knew what it was.

"Enough!" he shouted, losing his temper.

He reached out, grabbing the flashlight mid-air.

She squealed in pain as he twisted the flashlight out of her grip. He heard a snap, as if a bone broke.

She was too much trouble. Too much trouble. Just deal with her now.

He shoved the gun's muzzle against her stomach. Pressed it in. Not much fat, but there was a little.

Pulled the trigger.

She didn't scream.

More of a grunt of pain. As if she'd been punched in the stomach.

Good. She was gone.

Her body slumped away from his, falling heavily against a shelving unit.

He had the flashlight in his hand. He shone it on her face.

There was still life there. But not much. There was a strange look in her eyes. He'd seen that look before in men and women that he'd killed.

Some people might wonder what that look meant. Some people might ponder about the meaning of the whole thing, about life and death. About killing. About murder.

But not Froggy.

He'd killed her.

That was that.

Time to move on.

He shone the flashlight's beam around the basement, looking for the staircase.

He found it.

He started making his way there, only tripping once on a bag of rice that had been torn open.

"Shit," he muttered, looking back at the woman he'd shot, shining the flashlight on her.

She was panting, moaning softly in pain.

Good. She'd suffer. That's what these people deserved.

Froggy picked himself up. Took his first step up the stairs. It creaked. But not loud enough for anyone to notice. Not over the din that was above him.

People on the first floor were screaming. Someone was pounding on a door. Or wall. Or window.

Glass cracked.

Perfect.

Froggy knew that his job would only be easier with chaos already afoot.

"He thinks he's not infected."

"I already told him he's wrong. There's no way he's not..."

"I don't know where he got these ideas. Says we're killing him by kicking him out of the house. Says the whole virus thing is a big scam. A government trick. Some kind of trap. Or some crazy media thing. I don't know."

Matt watched Judy's face carefully in the low light. A flashlight beam was pointed towards the ceiling, resting tail-end down on a sturdy table , providing a little ambient light.

Judy's face showed the emotional pain she was in.

Matt had been impressed with how she'd handled the situation so far. Impressed that she'd been able to kick her own son out of her house.

But now, was she starting to break? Was she starting to crack?

Were the emotional and instinctual demands of motherhood taking a hold of her?

Would she demand that they let him back in?

"We can't let him back in, Judy," said Matt, speaking calmly and careful.

"I know. I know. He's going to kill us all."

"If he hasn't already."

The banging on the window had intensified. Now it sounded like he was using a rock.

Then came the sound of shattering glass.

"He's broken the glass."

Matt tightened his grip on his Glock.

"You've got to do it for me, Matt," said Judy, suddenly looking him dead on in his eyes. "I know that it needs to be done... I know I should do it... but I just can't..."

There was no need to discuss what she meant by "it."

It was clear.

Someone needed to shoot Damian.

Matt just nodded. There wasn't much to say. It had to be done, not talked about.

Matt stood up.

"He's almost inside," cried out Jamie from the other room. There was panic in her voice.

Matt walked swiftly in her direction.

He didn't run.

He needed time to think this over. Time to convince himself that it had to be done.

He already knew it had to be done.

They'd tried talking Damian out of it. They'd tried telling him to go back to the shed. They'd tried everything, but words hadn't made an impact.

It was time for force.

Deadly force.

Would it be the hardest thing that Matt had ever had to do, shooting his friend?

He didn't know.

He did know that nothing he'd ever done had prepared him for this. Sure, he'd gone to the range. He'd read the right books and watched some highly sought-after instructional videos. They'd discussed the mechanics. They'd discussed strategy.

But they hadn't discussed emotional situations. Situations in which it was hard to do the right thing. Situations in which every part of your instinct told you, screamed at you, not to take the actions that you knew were crucial to your survival.

Matt's fear was that he'd freeze up. That he'd just stand there, doing nothing, unable to pull the trigger.

He entered the room.

Jamie was back against the wall opposite the window. Gun in her outstretched hands. Finger on the trigger.

But she couldn't do it.

She'd worked with Damian. She knew him. It was too much.

Maybe if Damian got inside, she'd do it.

But Matt didn't need to put her through that.

He'd do it. Get it done with.

Jamie was shining a flashlight on Damian's face, illuminating it in an eerie, horrible way.

"You!" screamed Damian, his words coming out like a terrified hiss. A horrible sound.

The glass pane was shattered. Damian had stuck his head through the glass.

His face was bright red, as if his blood pressure was high.

It was a disturbing sight.

He looked deranged. His eyes were wide. Something was strange with his pupils. His eyes looked bloodshot. Veins on his forehead bulged.

Glass shards dug into his face. He seemed not to care. He

seemed disoriented, trying to get his whole body through what was a tiny window pane.

He could have gotten through the window if he'd punched out all the glass. But he was approaching it like an animal. A sick animal.

"One last chance, Damian," said Matt, his voice ringing out loud and clear.

"Screw you," hissed Damian. "It's my house!"

Matt raised his gun. His arm was outstretched, finger now on the trigger.

He opened his mouth to mutter the single word, "sorry," but then he thought better of it.

He wasn't sorry.

And this wasn't hard.

It was what he had to do.

It was either live or die. That was the only choice.

And he chose to live.

Matt pulled the trigger. The Glock kicked.

Damian's face took the bullet. His face imploded. A bloody mess. Disgusting in every respect.

Damian fell back, the glass tearing at his destroyed face.

Matt couldn't believe he'd done it. He didn't feel guilt. Maybe just a pang of it.

Instead, he felt relief. Stunned relief.

He didn't lower the Glock. Kept his arm outstretched, in case Damian reappeared.

But he didn't. And Matt stood there.

"Drop the gun, and turn around slowly," came a voice. A male voice. A weird accent. Kind of thick. "Either that, or I blow the little lady's head clean off."

Matt's ears were ringing, making the voice sound muted. But he could still hear it.

Matt acted instinctively.

He disobeyed the orders. He spun around, pointing his Glock in the direction of the new voice.

A rough-looking guy, tall and lanky, was holding Jamie against him. One hand clutched a handgun. The other arm was draped around Jamie's neck, a long knife pressed into her neck.

How did he get in here?

The man sneered. Fired his gun.

A gunshot rang out.

Glass behind Matt shattered.

A miss.

Matt exhaled slowly. A thin stream of air. Just like he did at the range. He tracked the man's head. Got it just right. As good as a shot as he was going to get.

It was all happening within the span of a single second.

There wasn't any time to think.

Just act.

Matt pulled the trigger.

The Glock kicked predictably.

But it was a miss. The bullet struck the papered drywall behind Jamie and the man. Bits of the drywall exploded outwards.

Matt's finger was pushing against the trigger, but he hesitated to fire again. He didn't trust himself now not to shoot Jamie in the head.

"Here you go, pretty," growled the man, suddenly jabbing the knife into Jamie's throat.

Matt acted. He didn't think about it. He just dashed forward, planning on tackling the man before he could get the knife all the way through Jamie.

Maybe Matt would die in the process. Maybe not. But at least he wasn't likely to kill Jamie.

Matt's arms pumped at his sides. His shoes slammed into the wood floor.

But before he could get to the two of them, the man's face had exploded outwards, part of his head still intact, in a general sort of way.

The man's body fell heavily and quickly to the floor. Landed with a thud.

Judy stood behind him, a wide stance, gun in both hands, arms outstretched.

It was a good shot. No time to congratulate her. Jamie was bleeding from the neck.

"You still with us?" said Matt, kneeling down, putting his arms around her.

The knife had fallen to the floor, but there clearly a wound in her neck. Blood flowed freely from it.

"Was he Australian?" she said.

"What? What's my name? Are you delusional?"

"I'm not delusional. And I'm not dead. It's just his accent was strange... what do you think, British or Australian?"

Matt didn't know what to make of this strange line of questioning. But he was glad that Jamie was still alive.

Maybe she was speaking oddly due to the stress. He'd heard of things like that.

He explored the gouge in her neck with his fingers. It was superficial. Nothing serious.

"You're going to be fine," he said.

"He's definitely from Australia," she was saying.

"Shut up," snapped Judy suddenly. "I heard something in the street."

Just what they needed. More noises. More possible threats.

The three of them waited in the dark room.

There was blood all over Matt's hands.

The light was dim. Very dim.

There was nothing but silence.

Matt could hear his own heart beating wildly, as if it were an animal escaping a predator, galloping across the plains.

Matt's eyes fell on the dead man. His face was no in no way intact, but the surrounding areas of his skull were.

It was a horrifying sight, but Matt couldn't look away. His eyes traveled up from the empty space where the face had been to the forehead.

There was blood everywhere. And bits of flesh and skin. And some bone.

Then Matt saw it.

The veins.

The enlarged veins on the neck.

No.

It couldn't be.

If that man was infected, then it seemed like he and Jamie would definitely be infected.

How could they not be? They were so close to his body.

Matt looked over at Jamie, and he saw that her eyes had seen the same thing.

"Infected?" she whispered so quietly it was more like she was mouthing the words.

Matt's eyes traveled down the corpse to the hands. The corpse's arms were at odd angles. One of the hands was positioned so that he could see the back of it.

The veins on the back of the hand were clearly enraged. Extremely dilated. There was no way he wasn't infected.

"Judy," whispered Jamie. "We've got a problem."

"Shhh," hissed Judy.

The three of them fell silent again.

Seconds ticked by.

A full minute passed.

Suddenly, there was a knock on the door.

"Was that...?"

It seemed improbable. Even impossible.

Who would be knocking in the door?

"Sandy? Are you in there?" came a loud, booming voice that was incredibly deep.

Sandy? Who the hell was that?

Another knock. More of a pounding this time.

Then came the actual pounding.

Someone was pounding on the door. It was unmistakable.

"Shit," someone muttered.

It didn't matter who. The sentiment was the same no matter what.

They were probably infected.

And now someone else was coming for them?

How much could they take.

Matt gripped his Glock tighter.

He could take it.

He had to.

J amie's mind was reeling. She could barely believe what had happened.

And now there was just more of it.

Reason had gone out the window. Reason had been burnt at the stake. Reason had gone up in flames too many times to count.

There were no reasons any more. No motivations.

None of that mattered.

What mattered was that they were alive. Some of them, at least.

"We've got to get upstairs," said Judy. "The door won't hold for long. It's already off its hinges. It's just furniture at this point..."

"You think there are a lot of them?"

"By the sound of it."

"What do they want?"

"Doesn't matter. It's just all violence at this point. They'll kill us. There are no reasons any more."

"Come on. We can hold them off at the staircase... it's narrow..."

"Mia!" said Jamie, suddenly remembering Mia. "I've got to get Mia."

"Hurry," hissed Matt. "Judy, you head upstairs. I'll wait by the door." He was whispering, clearly not wanting to risk that possibility that the enemy would overhear him. "I'll take the first one out... then I'll hightail it up the stairs with you..."

"The second one will get you. It's not safe."

"The whole situation isn't safe. Trust me, I got this."

"If we lose you, we're going to die."

"We might already be dead. Remember the virus."

Jamie had her gun in her hand. She was out of earshot of the conversation now. She was rushing through the hallways of the house.

The pounding on the front door was intense. Incredibly intense. It sounded almost as if someone was pounding something right on her own skull. That's how loud and intense it was in the darkness.

She felt nothing but fear. No hope. Nothing good remained.

"Mia!" she called out, reaching the top of the stairs. She didn't care if anyone heard her. It didn't matter. "Mia!" she yelled.

There was no answer.

Shit. She'd have to head downstairs.

She shone the light. Took her first step.

There was air coming in. A cool night breeze. What had happened? Why was air coming in?

She went down the stairs as quickly as she could.

At the bottom, she let out a scream.

A scream of fear. Surprise. Horror.

Her flashlight beam had found Mia's bloodied body.

"Mia!"

She rushed to her friend and roommate. Got her arms around here. Pulled her close.

The body was still warm. But there was no pulse.

Mia was dead.

"Mia..."

It must have been that man who'd broken in. He'd killed her. He'd shot her.

Suddenly realizing that she might not be alone, Jamie started shining the flashlight around the basement, jerking it around fanatically, following the beam of light with her gun.

There was no one else there.

Just her dead roommate.

Her flashlight beam found the shelves that had the supplies on it.

Something had happened to the supplies. Someone had torn into the bags. Thrown them everywhere. Scattered rice all across the floor. Semi-liquid coconut oil flooded the floor, a huge oily mess.

It was a complete mess.

On closer examination, Jamie found that all the food had been destroyed.

"You ripped up all the packages, Mia?" said Jamie, speaking to her dead roommate. She felt anger rising in her chest. "What the hell? Were you that messed up, or did you just not want us to survive?"

For all Jamie knew, it wasn't going to matter. The pounding on the front door was audible even down here in the basement.

She needed to get back upstairs. And quick.

Who knew how long that door would hold out.

And while it wasn't possible to get a straight shot to the

door from the staircase, one had to walk by the front door in order to get up the staircase.

If that front door broke before Jamie made it upstairs, then she could just forget about trying to get upstairs.

She turned on her heel and darted up the stairs.

She made her way through the hallways, racing so fast that occasionally she slipped and her body slammed into a wall. She ignore the pain and kept going, as fast as she could.

"Get upstairs," hissed Matt, barely whispering the words.

He was there near the door. Gun in both hands.

He'd dropped a flashlight in a corner. Some of the ambient light shone on the door.

The furniture that had been piled up behind the door was in complete disarray. It had been moved quite far.

The door was about to open. About to simply fall away, revealing dangerous invaders.

She wanted to stay. She wanted to help Matt.

But fear got to her. Fear of messing up Matt's plan. Fear of getting in the way. Fear of not being able to do what she had to do, like what had just happened with Damian.

Why hadn't she been able to shoot him?

She should have done it.

She needed to have done it.

She was weak.

And she felt weak as she darted up the stairs.

"In here," hissed Judy, a light appearing down the hallway.

Jamie didn't need to be told twice. She dashed through the open doorway, nearly tripping over Judy's leg.

Jamie stumbled, but recovered her balance, just as a gunshot echoed from downstairs.

One shot.

Then another.

Then a third.

Then silence.

Jamie's heart was pounding. It was all she could hear. Her ears were ringing.

She looked over at Judy, trying to read her expression.

Had the shot been from Matt? From the invader?

The furniture had moved. The door had opened.

Or more accurately, the door had simply fallen away from the frame.

A torso had come through, arms and legs seeming to follow.

Matt didn't try to make sense of it. He'd just pulled the trigger. His plan had been simple. All he'd had to do was stick to it.

A body had fallen away.

Only to be replaced with another.

Matt sent two bullets into the second body.

But, as he did so, a third and fourth person had made their way through the open door.

They were like ants. Like insects who didn't seem to care if they lived or died. They just kept coming. Like a plague. Like some horrible infestation.

This was the weak point in Matt's plan. Why had he believed that he'd be able to make it upstairs?

He'd only had time to half turn around, before someone was mere feet away from him.

He'd never make it up the stairs, let alone anywhere near it.

Something swung towards Matt's head. Matt pulled the trigger, but there wasn't time to aim.

The bullet went somewhere. Not into his attacker.

Matt's ears were ringing.

Matt ducked down.

He saw a flash from the object swinging at him. A flash of light reflecting off the metal from the flashlight he'd tossed on the floor.

It was a metal baseball bat.

It missed his head, but smashed into his shoulder.

Hard.

Pain flared through him.

Matt grabbed the bat with one hand, yanking it as hard as he could.

But the other man was stronger, pulling the bat back and away from Matt. It slipped through his hand.

The bat was coming back at him.

There were more people in the doorway. More people coming in. How many of them were there?

Matt's arm didn't seem to be working right. The pain was too much. Something had happened to more than just his shoulder.

Hard to aim his gun.

But he shifted his body, getting the muzzle of the Glock so that it lined up with the body.

Squeezed the trigger.

The Glock kicked.

More of a roar in his ears.

Matt didn't wait to see what happened. He turned on his heel.

Dashed towards the stairs.

He didn't think he'd make it. There were too many of them. Pouring through the door like water.

But he got to the first step. Foot on it. Then the second. Dashed up the stairs.

A hand grabbed him. A strong hand with a good grip.

Matt twisted and turned, got out of the grip.

He'd never pushed himself so hard in his life.

He could barely see. Nothing but a tunnel of dim light in front of him.

Nothing in his awareness except the steps.

He was practically on all fours, climbing the staircase like an animal, with the Glock held against his palm.

Noise behind him. Grunts and growls. A scream of pain heard somehow above the roar in his ears.

In front of him, there was a sudden flash of light. Another gunshot ripping through the air. The sound intense. Brutal, even.

He'd seen a muzzle flash. Right in front of him.

How was he still alive?

His mind didn't understand what had happened.

Another flash of light.

It seemed as if he was deaf now. A dull roar of what felt like silence washed through his skull.

He could barely see.

His vision was washed out.

Something grabbed his ankle. Grabbed on tight.

Impossible to shake the grip. He kicked his leg. No use. The hand clung to him.

He was getting dragged down. Pulled back down the steps.

They'd tear him limb from limb if they got him. They'd bash his skull in.

At least he'd gotten a couple of them.

J udy had realized Matt wasn't going to make it. She'd dashed to the head of the stairs, where she'd stood in a good stance, waiting, arms outstretched, finger on the trigger.

Matt was climbing the stairs like an animal. Good. It gave her a chance to shoot down and over his head.

She took the opportunity.

Pulled the trigger.

Kept pulling it.

Kept the gun in a good grip.

She knew what she was doing. She knew how to keep it steady through the kickback. She knew what to expect.

She was surprised at herself. She felt nothing as she emptied her gun methodically, as she pumped bullets into the invaders.

No emotion at all. Nothing but quiet, calm triumph that echoed through her.

She shone her flashlight down over the staircase, the eerie path of white light illuminating all in a grisly, hyper-realistic way.

They were dead. All of them.

Sure, a couple of bodies twitched.

There were still some grunts of pain. But they barely sounded human.

Stretching down the stairs, there were bodies. And there was blood.

At the bottom of the stairs, it was a pile of furniture, the door, and more bodies. More blood. A tangle of limbs. Some vomit. Some guts.

Judy, for some reason, felt a calm wash over her. A strange sort of violent calm.

Her son was dead. She remembered that. There was nothing she could do to undo that. It was just a fact.

"Matt," she said, stretching her hand down to Matt, who was at her feet, below her on the staircase. "Come on. It's over."

Matt looked up at her, the flashlight in his eyes, casting strange shadows on his face.

He took her hand, and she helped pull him to the top of the stairs.

He stood there on the landing, turning his head around, looking at the bodies.

"It's over," she said again. "The ones that aren't dead have fled. We killed too many of them... they got scared."

But Matt didn't seem to hear her. Either he was in a state of mild shock or his hearing wasn't working from all the gunfire.

It was over.

All over.

For now, at least.

It was hard to understand. Hard to wrap her mind around what had happened.

She ended up staying there, at the top of the stairs,

looking down at the front door with her flashlight trained on it, trained on the bodies.

She and Matt stayed like that until the sun came up and a new day had started.

The hours of the night had left a lot of time for reflection, and it seemed as if her son's life flashed before her eyes as she sat there in the darkness, staring at the corpses. Memories of him as a little boy, as a middle-schooler. Memories of his prom. Memories of his first job after school. Memories of him failing out of college for the first time.

She tried to shake the memories, but she didn't know whether they'd ever leave her.

And she didn't think that she wanted to leave the memories behind anyway.

With the sun up, Judy, Matt, and Jamie sat together in one of the upstairs bedrooms. It was the room that Damian had been staying in. His things were still all over the floor. Somehow, it didn't bother Judy. Instead, it comforted her.

"Mia's dead," said Jamie, her voice sounding hollow.

Judy didn't know what to say. She just felt more of that hollow feeling that came up when she thought of her son.

Matt didn't know what to say either apparently. He just started nodding, a strange look in his eyes.

"She destroyed all the food," added Jamie. "She tore up the packages. I think she was just too messed up on the drugs... she didn't know what she was doing..."

"We still have the food in the freezer and refrigerator... some in the kitchen," said Judy.

"The power's out," said Matt. And it was. They'd tested it, and it was definitely off. And cell phone service was down as well. "The food isn't going to last that long."

"I don't know if we can stay here anyway," said Judy.

"That front door's not going to work for us. It's not going to keep anyone out, no matter how much furniture we pile up in front of it."

"I might be able to get it back on its hinges," said Matt. "Or attach it there somehow, but I think the real question is more about whether or not staying here is a good idea at all, even if we have a functioning door and plenty of food."

"Which we don't," said Jamie.

"Right."

"What are you thinking, Matt?" said Judy.

"I'm thinking that it's not a good time to be in the city," said Matt. "New Mexico is one of the least populated states in the country, but that's a meaningless statistic when you're in a city. It's just as densely populated here as a city in New Jersey... there are plenty of people here... plenty of people that are going crazy from stress... plenty of people willing to commit violence to get what they think they need..."

"So what are you saying? Where are we going to go if it's not here...?"

"Head out towards Santa Fe," said Matt. "There's plenty of open land between here and there... plenty of hills to get lost in..."

"But how will we survive?" said Jamie, her voice seeming to fill with terror at the thought of being out in nature, out in the natural world.

"We'll have to figure it out," said Matt. "There are animals to kill and eat... gas stations along the way to take supplies from... I think our chances are better out there than here... It's only going to get worse..."

"But isn't everyone going to die off?" said Jamie. "From the virus? You said it yourself, I thought. In a couple days' times, more than half the city is going to be dead."

"Yeah," said Matt. "But the people who remain alive are

going to be the nastiest, the most violent, the most vicious, the most brutal...."

"In short, the people that are going to pose the biggest threat to us, right?" said Jamie.

"Yeah," said Matt, nodding. "Judy, what do you think?"

"I think you're right," said Judy, taking her time and choosing her words carefully. "It's going to be tough to get out of the city. It's going to be an escape. But we've got to do it. If yesterday has taught me anything, it's that we're not going to last a week here in this house, or even in this city..."

"Right," said Matt, nodding. "I'd say we have about a fifty-fifty shot of making it out of the city and getting into the high desert... If we can do that, we've got a unique opportunity... if we were somewhere else in the country, then we wouldn't have anywhere to go... we shouldn't stand a chance."

"What do you think is happening all over the country?" said Jamie, speaking in a low, hushed voice.

Matt shrugged. "Probably the same thing as here. No point in worrying about it. If the National Guard comes in on their white horses, though, I'm not going to be complaining. But I'm also not going to hold my breath..."

"All right," said Judy. "We'll leave today, if we can. We'll take my car."

"We might have to walk," said Matt. "For all we know, the streets are still jam-packed with cars... nothing but cars wall to wall..."

"We'll take my car as far as we can then," said Judy. "And we'll plan to walk. Now I may be old but don't worry about me. I can keep up with you two..."

"There's one thing we're forgetting," said Matt, his voice somber.

"What?" There was anxiety in Jamie's voice.

"The virus," said Matt. "All our plans are well and good, but if we've been contaminated, we're dead."

There was silence on the landing.

Dead silence.

Jamie broke it first. After about a full minute. "You think we got contaminated?"

Matt shrugged. "One of us might have," he said. "I was in pretty close proximity to those guys downstairs... if I was going to get it, I'd have it by now. And unfortunately that'd mean that you two have it as well.... I don't think our chances are good..."

"What should we do then?"

Jamie seemed almost beside herself.

Judy, on the other hand, didn't feel much of anything at all. Maybe it was having been through the shock of losing her son already. Maybe she'd been expecting something like this all along, in the back of her mind.

"If one or two of us have it," said Judy. "The other might not yet have it... In all the commotion, I guess we'd forgotten about the risk..."

"It'd be pretty hard to keep everything just the right way," said Matt. "The risk of contamination wasn't our biggest concern... not with ten men trying to break into the house... We did what we could. I was thinking about the possibility of us breaking off and waiting out the time in three separate rooms, but realistically..."

"If one of us has it, the other two already do," said Judy, finishing his sentence for him.

"Right," said Matt. "And we're just going to be wasting time sitting around here... waiting to see if we've been infected..."

"You're saying just get a move on it already?" said Judy.

"Yeah," said Matt, nodding. "Just ignore the risk of contamination for now. Sitting around and waiting to see if we're infected is going to be too much stress anyway. Might as well stay active. So we get ready to go. We head out. See if we can make it out of the city, and then..."

"And then...?"

"And then if we've been infected, we take care of it. If we haven't, we keep going."

"What do you mean by that? By taking care of it?" said Jamie.

"I mean taking the easy way out," said Matt. "It's the responsible thing to do. We don't want to be a risk to others after we're infected. We'll discuss the plans once we get in the car."

Jamie shuddered. The thought of "taking care" of herself was too much for her.

It wasn't too much for Judy. It was the only plan that made sense. She wasn't going to go out the way her son did. She didn't believe in suicide as a rule. It wasn't moral, at least as far as she was concerned. But in situations like this, then it easily could be the only path. After all, she didn't want to be responsible for more death herself, by accidentally contaminated someone else in her desperation.

"It'll probably take us about half a day to get ready," said Matt, looking down at his watch. "Let's try to be in the car by noon."

"So we're going to spend the next five or six hours busting our butts," said Jamie. "Not knowing if we're going to even be alive in twelve hours? That sounds horrible."

"Welcome to our new lives," said Matt, glancing down the staircase at the corpses that littered the front hall. "This is our reality, whether we like it or not."

27

I t took longer than they'd thought for them to gather up the supplies in the house.

Much longer.

Matt kept glancing at his watch throughout the day, watching as the hours rolled past.

There were many reasons that it took longer than expected to get ready to leave.

For one thing, there were bodies all over the house. And something either had to be done with them, or they had to be walked over and around.

They chose the latter option, not wanting to come into any more contact with the bodies than they had to.

The other reason was that Mia had really done a number on the food stores below.

There were many things that might be useful in the basement, but it was difficult to get to them. For one thing, the basement was horribly messy.

It also just simply took a lot of time to hunt down items in the house. Judy often had an idea of where something was but wasn't quite sure. Some things she hadn't seen in years, like the hatchet that she swore was out in the shed, but turned out to be in an upstairs closet.

The three of them all worked together, but Judy, being a couple decades older than Matt and Jamie, got tired and occasionally had to take rest periods.

As they worked, there was a sort of unspoken tension between the three of them. They all had tacitly agreed not to speak about the very real possibility that they were all going to be dead within a day. There was the very real possibility that they were all infected.

There was also the possibility that something else would happen, that they'd have to face more violence very soon. If the violence didn't arrive at the house before they managed to leave, then certainly they'd encounter violence on the way out of the city.

It was almost to Matt's surprise when they'd finally gotten the car packed up and nothing had happened.

No one else had come to the house. No one else had attacked them.

In fact, no one else had even driven down the street.

The neighbors either seemed to have not gotten home from work, or to be hiding in their basements.

The sun had a few more hours left in the sky, and they were finally ready.

The car was packed.

Not just packed, but packed strategically.

They were well aware of the very real possibility of having to leave the city on foot. Therefore, they'd managed to improvise luggage that could be carried easily enough on foot, should they have to abandon the car.

Of course, it'd be better if they could bring the car with them. For one thing, many of the heavier unwieldy items would help them survive out in the high desert.

Packing had kept them busy. Kept their thoughts busy.

For a few hours, Matt had actually forgotten that they were probably all infected.

So when he saw Jamie standing there, staring at the backs of her hands, he cursed silently to himself.

And the next thing he did? Immediately looked down at the backs of his hands.

He expected the veins to be enlarged. Horribly enlarged. So enlarged that there was no doubt about his death sentence.

But to his surprise, they looked absolutely normal.

There was no mistaking it. They were the same as ever. Not in the least bit enlarged.

"They're... normal," said Jamie.

"Mine too," said Matt.

"What about yours, Judy?"

There was a long pause.

"Normal," she said.

"What does this mean?" said Jamie. "Surely we must have gotten contaminated... I mean those corpses alone... half of them have enlarged veins..."

"No idea," said Matt, shrugging. "Maybe we're immune."

"Immune?"

"Remember when the black death wiped out two-thirds of Europe?"

"No."

"Well, you know what I mean, though."

"Yeah. I know what you mean. But what about it? Why bring it up? You think that many people will die now?"

"No idea," said Matt. "But what I do know is that some people exposed to the plague were immune."

"They were?"

"Yeah, and no one knows why."

"They never figured it out? Even scientists today?"

Matt shook his head. "Nope," he said. "Usually the immune were the ones who ended up carting the bodies of the dead around... they were the only ones who could do it without getting sick and dying themselves... they figured it was an act of God..."

"Maybe it was."

Matt shrugged.

"You think it's a similar situation?"

"What?"

"The black death. The plague."

"Maybe," said Matt. "The big difference is that there are a lot more people now... the population is many times that of medieval Europe... and society is more complex... much more reliant on technology... and all the technology seems to have failed us..."

"Right," said Jamie, holding up her cell phone. "This is basically useless now without the networks functioning."

"You drive," said Judy, checking over a backpack she carried one last time. She tossed the car keys to Matt, who caught them.

"Right," said Matt, opening the driver's side door of Judy's sedan. "Judy, do you want to... I don't know... say goodbye?"

"To my son?" said Judy, shaking her head. "No. I already have. In my own way."

Matt nodded.

Jamie gave Matt a look. He didn't know what it meant.

He lowered himself into the driver's seat. Closed the door behind him. Hands on the wheel.

The suspension of the sedan sagged a bit as Jamie and Judy got into the car.

Judy rode in the back, Jamie in the passenger's seat.

"Everyone ready?" said Matt.

Nods and murmurs of agreement.

Matt put the key in the ignition. Cranked the engine.

It fired right up. Had a good, healthy sound to it.

The car wasn't anything fancy. But it worked. And that's all they needed now.

Matt didn't know what would happen. He didn't know what the next day would bring, let alone the next week. He didn't even know what was around the next corner.

But what he did know was that he'd do everything he could to survive.

And he knew that his chances of surviving were better than they would have been if he'd been alone.

Damian and Mia had paid the ultimate price. They hadn't been prepared. But more importantly, they hadn't had the right attitude. They hadn't been mentally tough enough.

Thousands would die. Probably thousands already had.

If there was one thing Matt was sure of, it was that he was going to do everything he could to be one of the ones who lived. And he was taking Jamie and Judy with him.

READ MORE of my books here: https://www.amazon.com/Ryan-Westfield/e/B075MXJJ49

SIGN up for my newsletter to hear about my new releases. http://eepurl.com/c8UeN5

ABOUT RYAN WESTFIELD

Ryan Westfield is an author of post-apocalyptic survival thrillers. He's always had an interest in "being prepared," and spends time wondering what that really means. When he's not writing and reading, he enjoys being outdoors.

Contact Ryan at: ryan@ryanwestfield.com

Get updates about new releases by following Ryan on Facebook: https://www.facebook.com/ryanwestfieldauthor/

ALSO BY RYAN WESTFIELD

Getting Out (The EMP, book 1)

Staying Alive (The EMP, book 2)

Pushing On (The EMP, book 3)

Surviving Chaos (The EMP, book 4)

Fighting Rough (The EMP, book 5)

Defending Camp (The EMP, book 6)

Getting Home (The EMP, book 7)

Finding Shelter (The EMP, book 8)

* * *

Final Chaos (Surviving, book 1)

Final Panic (Surviving, book 2)

Final Dread (Surviving, book 3)

.